She knew how dangerous he was!

Call him Lord Roxbury, but never forget that he is really Charles Norton, despite the scar and his hair the years had turned dark, despite his dandyish airs and his preoccupation with his own importance; no one who had been kissed by him could forget the curve of that expressive, full-lipped mouth or the timbre of his deep voice. He was more alive than any man she had ever known.

And how she despised him!

TO LONDON, TO LONDON

Jane Hinchman

FAWCETT CREST • NEW YORK

A Fawcett Crest Book
Published by Ballantine Books
Copyright © 1984 by Jane Hinchman

Library of Congress Catalog Card Number: 84-10136

ISBN 0-449-21650-0

This edition published by arrangement with Doubleday, a division of
Bantam, Doubleday, Dell Publishing Group Inc.

Manufactured in the United States of America

First Ballantine Books Edition: March 1989

CHAPTER ONE

Laughter lurked in Caroline Hearn's blue eyes as she paused in the act of unpinning her thick gold hair to watch her cabin mate wrench open the porthole and fling an object into the sea.

"Let us hope it sinks, Aunt Dilly. You have left a guilty trail of bows and flounces halfway across the Atlantic."

Miss Dillon Hearn, a small woman of nearly thirty years whose upturned nose and flashing gray eyes proclaimed her independent nature, slammed the porthole shut and shook herself irritably.

"Matilda Sample always used three bows where one would have been too many. I regret that I agreed to wear her wardrobe, but your mother had already spent a great deal to have it made up and I hate waste of any sort."

"Are you finding it very unpleasant to act as my chaperone, Aunt Dilly?"

"Of course I am not. It is only having to use Matilda's name that I dislike. Simply because she caught a husband—who died as soon as he discovered what a bore he had married!—she was consid-

1

ered a suitable chaperone while I was not." An unladylike grin lightened her dainty features. "How like Matilda to contract a putrid fever when it was too late to find you another companion. She was ever a difficult female."

"Are you sorry you agreed to take her place?"

"No, I've made up my mind to enjoy this enforced visit to England. As for my duty toward you, Caro, I shall enjoy it. I consider you not only a sensible creature despite your eighteen years but lovely in every way. *You* wear laces and ruffles as properly as a plant blooms. On me they are an abomination!"

Even as she spoke, Miss Dillon Hearn, having spied a bow nestled in a cunning fold of lavender lace which she had overlooked, gave a crow of triumph. She clapped her hand over the unfortunate bit of fabric, gave it a twist, and captured it.

The gesture was too much for Caroline's equanimity. She could not restrain a gurgle of laughter. "It might have been a spider! Oh, Aunt Dilly, what fun we're going to have!"

"Not if you're to spend all your time at balls and routs in search of a titled husband." Miss Dillon Hearn retired behind a swaying curtain in a corner of their cabin and began to disrobe. "Your mama expects you to come home betrothed to no less than a baronet."

"Mama thinks I might aspire even higher considering the size of Papa's property." Caroline shook out the river of her golden hair. "I am not sure I want to marry yet, Aunt Dill. I'm not in a hurry to settle to doing needlework and attending tea parties with other matrons."

"Most women appear to enjoy domesticity," Dillon remarked from behind the curtain. "Your mama seems happy. Of course my brother has provided her with everything a woman could wish for, but I am persuaded that they are genuinely fond of each other, as well."

Pausing to strip off a stocking, Caroline smiled. Papa and Mama were famed for their devotion. Trust Aunt Dill to use the word "fond." To mention love would disturb her as deeply as to come upon another hidden bow.

"I believe they are, Aunt Dill," Caroline agreed. "Will you unhook me when you're ready for bed? I can't reach around, and poor Emerald is too ill to leave her cabin."

"Of course I will. I trust neither of us is too feeble to attend to our wants without the help of a maid!"

Her aunt emerged wearing a bedgown that enveloped her slender figure like a tent. Her thick brown hair was braided into two stern plaits, and she wore a pair of knitted slippers on her narrow feet. No doubt her years spent patrolling corridors at the Latin School, where she had served as assistant to the late Grandfather Hearn, had taught her to be prepared for any eventuality.

Caroline knelt. Her aunt began to unfasten tiny covered buttons and hooks. It was a time-consuming task.

"Aunt Dill, why did you never marry?" Caroline inquired pensively. "You are still quite pretty, and you are always so interesting to talk to."

For a second, fingers fumbled over a button.

"There was a man, but he went away. I've never met another one I liked as well."

3

"Was he someone I know? A friend of Papa's at the shipyard or one of his captains? They're all so handsome and dashing."

"He was not from Philadelphia. He let it be known that he was a younger son of a noble English family. When he disappeared overnight without leaving any word, no one doubted that he was simply a clever rogue."

"Perhaps he was recalled to England suddenly to assume the family title," Caroline suggested romantically.

"Had that been the case, he could have written," her aunt replied dryly. "There, you're undone. We'll speak no more of this matter." With a twitch of her voluminous bedgown, she climbed into her berth.

"Good night, Aunt Dilly. I hope I haven't upset you."

A rustle of covers and then, "Not at all. I never look back."

The *Artemis* ran into stormy seas the next day. Only a handful of her passengers gathered in the dining salon in the week that followed. Among them were Caroline and her aunt, who was known to those aboard as Mrs. Matilda Sample, widow.

A certain camaraderie began to grow among those who were not suffering from seasickness. Caroline made friends with a tall, dark-eyed young man named Courville, who was traveling to France with his father in order to discover whether any of their family had survived the recently ended Napoleonic Wars.

Dillon, after an interview with young Gilbert Courville, made up her mind that he was too quiet

4

and serious to pose a romantic threat to Caroline, so she agreed that the young people might take a daily walk around the deck where ropes had been strung for the sake of safety. Mindful of her duty, Dillon accompanied them regularly, even after she developed a cold that caused her to fall into violent spasms of sneezing from time to time.

To complicate matters, in Dillon's mind, was the fact that the young man's father persisted in walking at her side in spite of her cool responses to his efforts at conversation. She did not dislike him—quite the contrary—but he diverted her from her duty, and this she found hard to forgive.

One day, much to Dillon's fury, she slipped on the spray-swept deck, dangerously near to the railing. In a trice Mr. Courville had her by the arm and dragged her back to safety.

Dillon stood up and shook herself, her gray eyes flashing.

"I'm perfectly able to manage by myself, sir!"

Caroline and young Gilbert had come running back and now stood watching with solicitous expressions. Dillon fancied she saw the hint of a smile on Caroline's perfectly modeled mouth and at once drew herself up to the full extent of her five feet and two inches.

"You may depend on me to chaperone the young people as usual, Mr. Courville. You are quite free to return to your cabin."

"Surely you won't banish me out of hand! I am enjoying the fresh air," the elder Mr. Courville protested, his black eyes, so like his son's, twinkling merrily.

"If anyone is to retire, it had best be you, dear

Mrs. Sample," Caroline suggested. "This chill wind is not at all the thing for your cold."

"I find it extremely invigorating."

Dillon had hardly finished speaking when she was overcome by a hurricane of sneezing. Protesting when she could catch her breath, she was led inside, where a sympathetic steward offered several remedies, all of which proved unsuccessful. In the end she was forced to retire to her cabin. There, between sneezes, she fretted about having left Caroline alone with Gilbert Courville.

He was handsome in a fine-drawn way, well educated and agreeable, but Caroline was only eighteen and the boy far from the lordly match Caroline's mother, whose English cousins were to sponsor Caroline's London Season, envisioned for her beautiful daughter.

A fresh wave of sneezes attacked Dillon. She reached out blindly for something to hold on to. At the moment the *Artemis* slid into the trough of a great wave and wallowed sickeningly. Dillon felt her way to her berth and crawled in. Worry must wait.

Her face buried in her pillow, she was struck by a blinding memory that she had determined long ago to forget. Soft laughter and Charles saying, "Dare to sneeze again when I want to kiss you and I shall have to apply pressure . . ."

"I can't help myself. Please, Charles!"

He had his arms around her. Drawing back, he had looked down into her face and put the tip of his forefinger on the childish cleft in her short upper lip. As she looked at up him in surprise, he had bent and covered her mouth with his. Impossible then to sneeze! It was difficult even to remain standing, for her knees had turned limp, and she had clung to Charles in a haze of bliss.

Neither of them heard her father enter the parlor.

"Have you no shame, the two of you! Young man, leave my house at once. Dillon, go to your room."

"Sir, you don't understand. I love your daughter!"

"If that is true, why haven't you asked my permission to address her?"

Poor Charles. Under the stern blue glitter of Patrick Hearn's eyes he stumbled over his explanations. Because he was a younger son and only a junior naval officer, he was not yet in a position to marry, but, he said, Dillon had promised to wait until he gained promotion.

"Until you are in a position to marry, you have no right to trifle with my daughter's affections."

"Sir, if you will only give me time—"

Mr. Hearn went to the door and threw it open. Charles had no choice but to leave, but he looked back urgently and Dillon saw him form the words "the park, tomorrow."

A weaker woman might have shed a tear at the memory of the pain she had suffered during the ensuing afternoons of waiting for a man who never came back or sent word. Not Miss Dillon Hearn! Once again, she steeled her heart firmly against love—that foolish, irrational emotion she would never succumb to a second time!

The door opened to admit Caroline on a gust of salt wind.

"Not asleep yet, Aunt Dilly?"

"Hardly, under the circumstances. I trust that the senior Mr. Courville did his duty as chaperone after I was forced to retire."

"He did indeed, and I found him a most interesting gentleman. Did you know that he is an inventor? It was thanks to his newly invented cannon and gunpowder that we prevailed in the recent war with England."

"Thanks are due to men like your father as well. His ships and captains regularly outsailed the British."

"I know, but Mama warned me not to mention that to our English cousins."

"Naturally we must guard our tongues while we are guests of Lord and Lady Neville, but we need not be toadies! I, for one, mean to speak my mind frankly and fairly as always."

Caroline slipped behind the curtain to undress. As she hung up her petticoats, a task she was unused to doing at Hearn Hill, she experienced a wave of foreboding.

Aunt Dilly's mind was crammed with advanced opinions about every matter under the sun, from the lack of rights for females to such embarrassing problems as the best way to keep the growing population of the world in check. Heaven alone knew how she might react at tea parties where guests held strong opinions on the other side.

The real Mrs. Sample was a prosy, tiresome widow, but at least one could be certain she would never say anything out of the way.

Ah well. Caroline washed sketchily and lay down in her berth. There might be trouble ahead, but with Aunt Dilly, one was sure never to be bored!

The weather turned mild as the *Atremis* neared Ireland. Passengers long confined to their cabins emerged palely to take a turn on deck. It was not long before a wager was laid among the gentlemen that Gilbert Courville would offer for Miss Caroline before the voyage ended.

"She won't have him," one of the older men said. "With her beauty and a stake in the biggest ship-yards in America, she can aim as high as an earl. That lad's in for a setdown."

A similar train of thought occupied Dillon as she and her niece changed for dinner a few days before they were due to make port.

"I hope you have not encouraged Gilbert Courville, Caro. Or worse, that you haven't formed an attachment yourself. Remember that we will never see the Courvilles again after we land."

Caroline's lovely high forehead was serene and her blue eyes tranquil as she finished pinning up her golden curls.

"The Courvilles have promised to call upon us in London after they finish their business in France. But you needn't worry. Gilbert and I part only as the best of friends."

Dillon said a silent prayer of gratitude. Fonder of her niece than she would admit, she hoped nothing would occur to damage Caroline's naturally sunny disposition. Brought up in luxury, an acknowledged beauty since her earliest school days, Caroline had known nothing but love and approval. She hardly realized what it was to desire something she could not have.

And never will if I can help it, Dillon resolved.

She jabbed a dozen hairpins impatiently into the awkward structure of shiny light brown hair that passed with her as a coiffure and covered it with one of Matilda's hateful ruffled widow's caps.

A general air of celebration prevailed at dinner now that the end of their rough voyage was near. Seated beside the captain, Dillon carried on a lively discussion with him on the subject of celestial navigation. Turning to the gentleman on her other side, an elderly German philosopher who had suffered excessively from seasickness, she offered him sympathy in his own tongue and was chagrined when he seized her hand and kissed it fervently. What could she have said in her rusty German to have aroused his ardor? With relief she accepted an offer from the senior Mr. Courville to partake of chocolate in the main salon.

"I will be sorry when this voyage ends," Mr. Courville told her after they had discussed the weather and their probable time of arrival. His black eyes roamed around the salon. "As will my son, I am sure. He and Miss Hearn have become fast friends."

His words triggered an alarm in Dillon's mind. Where was the young couple? They had left the dining salon before the general exodus.

"They will have gone up on deck, depend upon it! Come along. We must not leave them alone together."

"Your coat . . ." Mr. Courville panted, trailing after her as she ran outside and up the stairs.

"Do come along and stop fussing."

In spite of their hurry they found the deck deserted after two trips fore and aft. Dillon halted and looked around her, shivering. "They *must* be some-where about," she worried.

"Perhaps they took shelter from the wind. Let us search the area under the lifeboats."

It was a sensible notion. Dillon followed Mr. Courville into the shadows where a spurious warmth did indeed exist. Kind Mr. Courville! She was convinced that he meant only to stop her shivering when he put his arms around her and enfolded her in a suffocating embrace until the moment when he declared that he loved her and desired above all things to kiss her.

"You forget yourself, sir! I am not that kind of woman."

"I never thought you were, Mrs. Sample. I am trying to ask you to be my wife. Nothing could be more fitting—you a widow and I a widower. Our ages are compatible, and I have learned to love and admire you during these weeks at sea."

"I have no wish to marry. That is, never again!"

Dillon pushed herself free of her admirer's arms and reached up to steady her pile of hair, which was threatening to fall down, as usual, thus giving Mr. Courville another opportunity to embrace her and plant a misplaced kiss on her left eyebrow.

"Release me, if you please. I do not enjoy being mauled about!"

"So. Your husband was a brute?"

She pounced on the excuse gladly. "I was most unhappy."

"With me you will have a very different life. My own first marriage was idyllic. I am convinced that I can make you as happy as was my dear Jacque-line."

"Mr. Courville, I shall soon be thirty. I am aware that I have no beauty and am far too outspoken to make any man a comfortable helpmate. Why in heaven's name do you wish to wed an aging spin—widow?"

"I find your lively mind stimulating. You are beautiful in your own way, Mrs. Sample. I apologize if I have frightened you by speaking too soon. Give me another chance. Let me have reason to hope, at least."

He had seized her hands and held them firmly. Though he was not tall, he was strong and determined. Dillon feared that he would never set her free unless she conciliated him. And she *did* like him a great deal, as a friend.

"I am flattered by your partiality to me, but I have vowed never to marry, sir. Never again, that is. Now if you will set me free, it is my duty to find my niece."

"Not until you say you don't dislike me!"

"It would have been a tiresome voyage without your company. Good night, Mr. Courville."

She pulled away and ran swiftly down to her cabin. Under no circumstances did she wish Caroline to catch her with tumbled hair and a look of having been kissed.

The cabin door stood slightly ajar. Dillon halted on the threshold in disbelief. Caroline was curled up in her berth in her bedgown directing the maid Emerald in the packing of her many trunks.

The *Artemis* lurched. Dillon clung to the door. Poor Emerald began to moan. Unperturbed, Caroline looked up and waved at her aunt with a cheerful smile.

Dillon glared. "If you pack with the notion of eloping with young Courville the minute we dock, let me assure you that I will never let it happen!

"Whatever gave you such a totty-headed notion, Aunt Dilly? I've made a mull of my clothes, and Emerald is trying to put them in order for our arrival in London."

The *Artemis* shuddered again as she encountered the turbulent Channel. Emerald dropped a bonnet and sank to the floor. "Oh, miss, it's in my throat again. I'll die sure this time."

Dillon staggered across to the washstand and brought back a cold cloth, which she applied to the forehead of the little Irish maid.

"You'll be fine as soon as you step on dry land. There, I've opened the porthole. Sit close and breathe deeply of the fresh sea air. Try to relax."

Obediently the girl closed her enormous eyes. Dillon went over and looked down at her niece, who appeared to be asleep, hands folded sweetly over the ruffled bosom of her bedgown.

"I know perfectly well that you're shamming, Caro. What have you done with that Courville boy?"

Caroline's lids flew open in innocent surprise.

"I haven't seen him since dinner. He told me his papa meant to ask you to marry him tonight, so we decided to leave you two alone." She sat up with an expectant grin. "Tell me all about it. Are you going to marry him? Gilbert says he would like you for a stepmama."

Dillon sank down on the side of the berth. "You dreadful children! If only you had warned me . . .

13

There I was, trapped beneath a lifeboat, never dreaming that Mr. Courville had expectations!"

"He's kind and clever and devoted to you. Are you sure you cannot like him?"

"Oh, I like him well enough. I simply do not feel toward him the way I should toward the man I would marry."

"It's time you forgot that scapegrace you fell in love with all those years ago, Aunt Dilly. You should be settled. Now that Grandfather is dead, you can't go on at the Latin School."

Dillon nodded unhappily. "The new headmaster has intimated that he can manage without me next year. Thanks to my investments in your father's ventures, I am more than comfortable financially. But I will miss my boys more than I can say."

"You're still young enough to have children of your own."

"Ridiculous!" Dillon jumped up and went across to the maid, whose pale face and damp forehead testified to her misery. "Come along, Emerald. I'll help you back to your cabin. Caroline can pack her own clothes if necessary. Lean on me, there's a good girl."

It was more than half an hour before Dillon returned to the cabin she shared with her niece and began to get ready for bed. Caroline lay quietly in her berth, waiting for her aunt to emerge from behind the curtain. "Forgive me if I've hurt you, Aunt Dilly," she murmured when she saw Dillon's reddened eyes as she bent to blow out her candle.

A sniff, a swish of bed covers, then silence was her only answer. Resigned to sleep unforgiven, Caroline was surprised to hear a gurgle of smothered laughter from the opposite berth.

"I've only just realized how neatly you turned the tables on me, Caro. If I have been too officious as your chaperone, I apologize. But don't dare play such a trick on me again."

"I won't. If you change your mind about nice Mr. Courville, let me know and I'll get the word to Gilbert."

"You wretched children! No more matchmaking, if you please!"

CHAPTER TWO

Miss Dillon Hearn, known in the Neville household as Mrs. Matilda Sample, huddled miserably between damp sheets like a forlorn small nestling and wished she had never left Philadelphia.

Emerald bustled through the door carrying a small tray, which she put down with an angry thump upon an unstable desk beside the bed.

"Lords and ladies they may call themselves, but they've no decent concern for their guests! The kitchen is in a dreadful derangle, Miss Dillon. Mrs. Sample, I mean. Beg pardon. I had to make a bit of gruel for you myself. I hope you'll eat it all for you're as skinny as an alley cat, as the lady in charge of the orphanage used to say to me."

"Has Miss Caroline wakened yet?" Dillon inquired hoarsely.

Her cold had descended to her chest and spread to her throat and ears. If she had had the least notion that the climate in London was so fickle she would have taken more time over her sight-seeing. Unfortunately, every time Caroline went off to the dressmaker or to attend a nuncheon or musicale

16

with Lady Neville, thus setting Dillon free, the rain came down in torrents. She had been drenched near London Bridge and almost drowned on the steps of Westminster Abbey without so much as an umbrella or a warm cloak.

"Awake, Miss Dillon! Why she was up and away to ride in the park with her new friend before ten o'clock."

"New friend?" Dillon leaned on one elbow anxiously.

"Miss Arabella Worthing. She came to tea last week. But if you ask me, it's not like Miss Caroline to get up betimes unless there's a man somewhere about, she being that beautiful they can't stay away from her. Or her them!"

"She may be forming an unsuitable attachment while I lie here as weak as a runt puppy," Dillon fretted. "Emerald, will you find Lady Neville and tell her I want to see her as soon as she has a moment to spare?"

"If I can, and *if* milady isn't too busy cosseting that precious son of hers or hiding the drink from her husband. They say in the kitchen that milady plans to marry Sir Mortimer to our Miss Caroline."

Dillon sat up so suddenly she spilled her chocolate.

"They are second cousins. It would not do at all!"

"Sir Mortimer has to marry an heiress, him and Lord Neville having sold up most of their property already."

"Emerald, you're becoming a dreadful gossip."

The girl's pretty round face turned pink. "I was only wanting to help because I'm so fond of you and Miss Caroline. It was Miss Caroline's papa that

17

chose me from all the other orphans and brought me home to wait on Miss Caroline. It felt like going to heaven when I came to Hearn Hill. Then you were all so good to me. Mrs. Hearn taught me how to go about being a lady's maid, and you gave me my Latin to go with the letters I learned from my dear Da before he died. There's nothing I wouldn't do for the Hearns, even to listening at doors if need be!"

"I'm grateful, Emerald." Dillon cleared her throat. "Come here and let me straighten your cap."

Emerald bent over the bed, her huge, starved-looking green eyes fastened on Dillon with trust and devotion. Dillon tucked in a stray black curl and patted the girl's cheek. "I'm glad we have you here with us, Emerald. Just go on keeping your eyes and ears open and let me know everything."

Dillon lay back on her lumpy pillows when the girl had gone and frowned at the mildewed bed hangings. So that was the game: the Nevilles planned to foist off their unsavory son, who was twenty but still weedy and afflicted with spots, upon their naive little cousin from America.

She had noticed before her illness that the Neville town house was shabby beneath a bit of surface freshening. Except when they entertained, which happened seldom, the food was scant and ill prepared. She had no doubt that they were using the money Caroline's father had provided in order to plump out their own wardrobes instead of giving parties for Caroline, for Dillon had heard nothing more of the ball they had promised to arrange in the girl's honor.

Indignation seethed in Dillon's breast and drove her to speak her mind when her hostess finally tapped at the door and entered just before noon.

"Lady Isabel, I own that I am not happy to hear that you permitted Caroline to ride in the park alone this morning!"

"She was accompanied by a groom. I did not forbid her ride since she was to meet Miss Arabella Worthing, who is the most desirable companion a visitor from the Colonies could hope for."

Lady Neville sank heavily into a worn tapestry chair beside the hearth, where a meager fire burned. A scrawny, amber-colored woman in her forties, Lady Isabel gave the impression that life had squeezed all the joy from her and left her dried as a raisin.

"Desirable? Do you imply that Miss Worthing is an heiress?"

"Unfortunately not. Poor Arabella's father died at Waterloo, but her pedigree is impeccable, and since she is Lord Roxbury's godchild, he has promised her a handsome portion when she marries. Arabella is quite lovely in her way, as dark as Caroline is fair. Mortimer says they have been dubbed the Heavenly Pair. He swears it is most difficult to win a word with either girl through their swarm of beaux."

That was a matter for which to give thanks, at least. Dillon inquired of Lady Isabel whether Caroline showed any special preference among the young men who called at the house regularly.

Lady Neville's muddy brown eyes blinked thoughtfully. "She and Mortimer have great fun together. Mortimer says she is a romp. Aside from him, she accepts the admiration she receives with exactly the proper air of being accustomed to it."

"That is only natural. There's not a man under thirty in Philadelphia who hasn't fallen in love with Caroline. But she says she is not ready to settle yet."

"Eighteen is not really young. If she is to have only this one Season she cannot afford to dally."

"There are any number of acceptable gentlemen in America she may marry, I assure you, Lady Isabel."

"No doubt, and yet I am sure her mother wishes her to marry into her own rank. Caroline's grandfather—dear Cousin Charlotte's father—was the youngest son. Since he had no expectations, he was sent to America to make his way. I believe he was never happy in the Colonies."

"I remember him well. He was perfectly content as long as he had a bottle of fine Madeira at his elbow."

"A taste for fine wine runs in the Neville family." A frown creased Lady Isabel's lined forehead. "My husband—ah well, we wives know how difficult it is to curb a gentleman's excesses, do we not?"

Dillon, recalling her role as Mrs. Sample, managed a sound she hoped would pass for agreement. But a moment later she burst out indignantly, "Why are we in such a hurry to marry off our daughters when we know how disagreeable marriage can sometimes be for a woman!"

Lady Isabel stared at her in surprise.

"But how much worse to condemn them to lonely lives as spinsters! Even though a husband may have his failings, he will give her children to comfort her."

Dillon clamped her lips shut against a tide of protest. Lady Isabel rose creakily. Though she was not yet fifty, she had aged prematurely. With a murmured wish for Dillon's speedy recovery and a promise to send one of her own remedies by the housekeeper, she took her departure.

Lying back on her knobby pillows, Dillon resolved never to let her niece enter on such a life. She fell into a doze and dreamed uneasily of a Caroline grown old and haggard while her English husband drank himself regularly into insensibility.

It was Caroline herself, rosy with excitement, who woke her up. "Such fun, Aunt Dilly. How I wish you had come with us! Arabella rides almost as well as you do. She's the only girl I've met who doesn't giggle as if she's fresh out of the schoolroom."

"You can't have been riding all this time. It's past noon already."

Caroline turned to hold her hands out toward the fire.

"We happened to meet Lord Roxbury, Arabella's godfather. He rode with us and afterward took us to visit his sister, Lady Pomfret. She gave us a delightful nuncheon. You must meet her when you are up and about again. Now I had better hurry and change. Lady Isabel is taking me to visit a friend."

"Perhaps you can spare me ten minutes later tonight?" her aunt inquired grimly.

Caroline halted at the door between their two rooms, her lovely face mischievous. "I only wish I might spend the entire evening with you, Aunt

Dilly. Mortimer and Lady Isabel are taking me to the theater tonight. The play may be interesting but—Mortimer! His lips are odiously damp when he kisses my hand. Oh, have no fear. I will behave, I promise."

She disappeared with a backward grimace. Dillon sat up and poured out a large dose of the horrid green medicine Lady Isabel had concocted. Unless she was poisoned, the bitter draught ought to put her back on her feet in a hurry.

She lay back and yawned and fell quickly into a deep sleep. When she awakened the next morning, she felt strong again and ready to do battle, although against whom she was not yet quite sure.

Five days later, Dillon sat watching as Emerald dressed Caroline in a high-waisted gown of golden gauze over a slip of pale gold satin. If it was unusual for a girl in her first Season to wear anything but pink, blue, or white, still the result was so perfect no one could find fault.

"Do you like it, Aunt Dilly?"

"You look like a Greek goddess come to life. You are bound to take Almack's by storm. Let us hope there are some gentlemen there of substance. I can't say much in behalf of the young men who have come calling on you at Neville House. Not a thought beyond the polish on their Hessians or the folds of a cravat! One wonders why they don't die of boredom."

Descending the staircase somewhat later, they were met by Mortimer and Lady Isabel. Mortimer declared himself struck dumb by Caroline's beauty, but he regained his powers of speech quickly when

22

he discovered that the carriage seat, where he was about to place his satin knee breeches, was dusty.

Lady Isabel beamed on him fondly after he finished rating the groom. "The Brutus arrangement of your hair is most becoming, Mortimer dear," she said.

The horses started forward. As the four people settled themselves, Dillon looked across at the young man curiously.

"What do you do, Mortimer?"

"Do?" He stared at her.

"I cannot believe you spend all your time attending parties. Do you look after the family estates?"

"That's m'father's affair, Mrs. Sample. On the unhappy day I inherit, I shall make certain all is in order, of course."

"In England it is not the custom for those nobly born to have useful occupations," Lady Isabel protested. "Matters of business are left to those trained to manage them. Surely it is no different in the Colonies?"

"I fear it is, Lady Isabel. Few of us have ancestors to bequeath us comfortable livings. Each man must make his own way."

"Good Gad, how does a fellow find time to hunt?" Mortimer cried.

Lady Isabel was even more perturbed. "Take care not to speak of such matters, Mrs. Sample. The slightest hint that Caroline's father has any connection with trade would ruin her chances of making a good match. Even though she is our cousin, I had great difficulty in obtaining vouchers for Almack's tonight."

"You are kind to me, Lady Isabel," Caroline murmured.

"I trust you will behave with discretion, child, for if you do not it will reflect upon all the Nevilles. Not that I find much to fault in your manners. In general you are pretty-behaved. It is only that in England young girls show more reserve. They do not laugh freely, nor offer opinions unless asked."

"Have I been an utter hoyden, Cousin Isabel? I fear it is in my nature to see the humorous side of events."

Mortimer rose gallantly to her defense. "It is impossible to be dull in Miss Hearn's presence!"

Their entrance at Almack's created a ripple of critical excitement. The patronesses and the assorted mothers and friends studied Caroline and her dowdy companion with cool reservation, but Caroline had no sooner been introduced than she was surrounded by a throng of young men clamoring for a dance with her.

"You will, of course, dance first with Mortimer," Lady Isabel instructed. "And remember that you may not waltz without permission from the patronesses. Perhaps another time I can arrange it."

Watching the proceedings as the evening went on, while Lady Isabel exchanged the latest on-dits with other mamas, Dillon decided that it was not so very different from a slave auction. Here she saw England's fairest daughters gathered for the purpose of being looked over as prospective wives while they did their best to catch husbands. Marriage portions were mentioned often, as were family pedigrees. The only thing the gentlemen didn't do was examine the girls' teeth, Dillon fumed, to verify their ages!

Mortimer brought Caroline back to her place, the first set having ended. Before the girl had time to seat herself, a tiny, vivacious, dark-haired beauty came running toward her, and they exchanged affectionate embraces while a circle of young men waited in the background.

"That is dear Arabella Worthing," Lady Isabel whispered to Dillon. "Roxbury's niece, you will recall. We've had cards for his ball in honor of Arabella next month."

"This Roxbury is a person of much consequence?"

"A hundred thousand a year, my dear! He had married a wealthy widow even before he came into his own inheritance, which is one of the largest in the kingdom."

"I am surprised that Lady Roxbury is not here with her niece."

"Lady Roxbury died in childbirth not long after they came back to England. She had lived in Jamaica, I believe." Lady Isabel fanned herself. "There is a son by her first marriage, but Roxbury has no heir of his own. He must marry, and yet he dallies about, spending his time on the Continent or visiting those dreadful places men frequent such as Cribbs Boxing Parlor . . ."

The two young girls were on the floor dancing the *boulanger*, Caroline with a tall young man Lady Isabel had said was Alsonett, a baronet, and Arabella with a handsome fair-haired man of serious deportment who looked upon his partner adoringly. "Sir John Huddleston," Lady Isabel whispered.

"Only a small competence and comes from an unimportant family. Lord Roxbury would never let him have Arabella."

Dillon listened as patiently as she could, stifling all the protests that rose to her lips. Her hated widow's cap began to tilt to one side above her untidy mass of brown hair. What am I doing here in Matilda's lacy lavender gown, she thought, playing a role for which I am not suited? If only she were at home in Philadelphia with a book to read and her cat Dante on her lap!

She spread out her fan to conceal a long yawn. Suddenly Lady Isabel grasped her by the wrist.

"Oh Lud! Here's Roxbury, come to Almack's after he swore he'd never spend another tiresome evening in the nursery again. There he is going across to Arabella. Now he is leading her out onto the floor. What a great honor for her! For all of us!"

Yawning again deeply, Dillon peered with watering eyes over her fan to catch a glimpse of the famous nonpareil. From the back he appeared well set-up, close to six feet in height, she judged. His head was massive upon a strong neck and wide shoulders. As he went down the line with Arabella, Dillon caught a glimpse of a jutting nose and a chin equally strong.

"Lord Roxbury is younger than I was led to believe," she said to Lady Isabel. "I thought he must be near fifty."

"He is closer to thirty-five, though he appears older owing to his experiences in the war with France. He sailed under Lord Nelson, and suffered wounds which . . ."

Lady Isabel's voice sank away as the object of

26

their interest passed close in front of them. Dillon saw him from the front for the first time.

It could not possibly be Charles Norton! This man's hair was brown, not ash blond. He had a slanting scar across his forehead, and he moved through the figures of the dance with a bored elegance wholly unlike the bouncy clumsiness of the Charles Norton she remembered, who could never avoid stumbling over the smallest object. Dante, the cat, always scrambled out of sight when he arrived, Dillon recalled, although he would sometimes condescend to sit on Charles's lap if coaxed.

The man she had fallen in love with had been alive with warmth and gaiety and not a cool sophisticate whose weary glance flickered over the assembled company with something close to disdain. Dillon clenched her hands and heard the sticks of her jet-trimmed fan snap.

He must be one of the older brothers Charles told me about, she assured herself. The heir. That would explain the uncanny resemblance as well as his haughty attitude.

The set came to an end. The dancers left the floor, Caroline and her partner walking beside Arabella and Lord Roxbury. With a sinking sensation in her middle, Dillon saw that they were coming toward the place where she sat with Lady Isabel. With a bow to Caroline, Lord Roxbury went away. As she acknowledged Caroline's introductions, smiling mechanically at Arabella, Sir John, and Caroline herself, Dillon saw Lord Roxbury cross the room and address Lady Jersey with easy familiarity. The patroness smiled up at him flirtatiously and punished his wrist lightly with her fan.

Caroline took the chair beside Dillon, after bidding an affectionate farewell to Arabella Worthing and her escort.

"The next dance is a waltz, and I am not yet allowed to dance it," Caroline confided to Dillon, her eyes sparkling. "Some of their customs are fully as quaint as they say ours are!"

"Indeed."

"Aunt Dilly, you look odd. Are you feeling not quite the thing?"

"I am perfectly well. It is only that I find it over warm in here." Dillon unfurled her limp fan and plied it vigorously, having spied Lord Roxbury part from Lady Jersey only to make his way back toward the corner where they sat.

Lady Isabel introduced him with flattering alacrity.

"Mrs. Sample." He bowed over her hand with polished deference and turned away to address himself to Lady Isabel. "May I have the waltz with Miss Hearn, Lady Neville. I have won Sally Jersey's permission so it is quite all right."

"Indeed not!" Dillon interrupted. "What of the other patronesses!"

Lady Isabel, flushing unbecomingly, put out a hand to Lord Roxbury. "You must forgive Mrs. Sample, sir. She is from the Colonies and unused to our ways. I give *my* permission. Nothing more is needed."

The music had already begun. With only a token bow, Lord Roxbury led Caroline onto the floor.

"It will not do. Caroline must be warned!" Dillon said urgently to Lady Isabel. If Lord Roxbury was a man like his brother Charles Norton, who had loved and deserted her, Caroline had to be protected from him.

"Of what, my dear lady? You are making a shameful pother over nothing!"

"Lord Roxbury is far too old and—experienced, if what you say is true, to seek out a girl as young as Caroline."

"Roxbury is at the right age to begin setting up his nursery with a young and healthy girl."

"How can you believe that he is serious? I am convinced that Lord Roxbury is amusing himself at the expense of my young, innocent niece!"

Lady Isabel's lip tightened. "My dear Mrs. Sample, every unattached female in England has set her cap for Roxbury. He has no need to dangle after a little Colonial, pretty though she may be."

Dillon had to bite back a sharp retort. So that was how Lady Isabel viewed her niece! She would have given years of her life to be safely back in Philadelphia as she sat and watched Caroline float gracefully around the floor in the arms of a man she believed to be full of guile and deceit.

Out on the floor, Lord Roxbury essayed a variation in the usual steps, which Caroline followed with perfect ease.

"So you are no stranger to the waltz?" He smiled down upon her, his darkly tanned face interested. "I am fortunate to have won such an accomplished partner."

"I have waltzed since I was fifteen, Lord Roxbury. One does not need permission to dance in Philadelphia."

"And have you always lived in that city, Miss Hearn?"

29

"My grandfather emigrated from Dublin when he was a young man. He was a notable scholar, and it was his dream to establish a school for gentlemen in a free country. Of course this happened before the . . . er . . . disagreement with England in 1776."

Lord Roxbury was not slow to catch the hint of amusement in her dulcet voice. "So you are tactful as well as beautiful. You are careful not to mention the fact that England has lost both her engagements with America. Dare I ask how your family regards the conquered foe?"

Caroline's lashes swept down on her cheeks demurely. "It is better not to inquire, Lord Roxbury. Consider me as an emissary bent on making peace between our nations."

"Had they sent you to negotiate, our recent war would never have been fought. Arabella informs me that you are already considered the Incomparable of this Season."

"Indeed not! It is Arabella who is beyond compare!"

"In that case, I assume you suffer qualms of envy."

Her mouth curved up at the corners irresistibly. "Not at all, sir. Between us, we plan to sweep the lists."

He raised his head and laughed so heartily that the seated mamas stopped exchanging gossip long enough to wonder among themselves what had caused his undignified behavior. The American, they whispered. Colonials were so lacking in decorum.

"Arabella tells me that you long to see something of the country. If it pleases you, I suggest that we arrange a picnic party to visit my estate at Botham Abbey. It is not much more than an hour from London. Parts of the Abbey are very old. You will enjoy examining relics of an ancient civilization."

Again the gleaming smile from Caroline. "I am well acquainted with several such relics. My Grandfather Neville was a melancholy example."

"As was your paternal grandparent, the one who emigrated from Ireland?"

Caroline's cheeks flushed at the hint of a sneer in his tone.

"Not at all. He was a man of brilliant intellectual attainments, an essayist and geographer as well as master of the Latin School."

"How praiseworthy," Lord Roxbury murmured in a suffocated voice.

The dance ended. He led her off the floor toward the row of chaperones. These ladies sat fanning themselves as they assessed their entries' chances in the matrimonial race for all the world like gentlemen at a racecourse, Dillon reflected grimly as she watched Caroline approach.

Lord Roxbury addressed himself to Lady Isabel. Though his back was not quite turned on Dillon, he managed to make it plain that she was excluded from their conversation.

"Since Miss Hearn longs to see something of the country, I have offered to arrange a picnic party for her and Arabella at Botham Abbey at a date convenient to you, Lady Isabel. Of course I will expect you and Lord Neville and Mortimer to be part of the company."

Lady Neville hesitated, anxiety and eagerness

fighting for preference on her worn face: anxiety lest Lord Roxbury cut out Mortimer in Caroline's affections, eagerness to become a part of the superior social world of Roxbury's circle.

Dillon took advantage of the pause to speak out firmly.

"Such an excursion is out of the question."

Lady Isabel turned pale, then flushed an angry red. "Why, nothing could be more delightful, Mrs. Sample, and it is perfectly proper so long as I accompany the girls! Since you are not invited, the matter need concern you no longer."

The bitter snub caught Dillon by surprise. She could think of several replies, none of them proper or polite. Not so Caroline.

"If Mrs. Sample is not going, then neither am I!"

"In that case, we must include your chaperone," Lord Roxbury agreed indifferently.

Dillon sat up very straight. "How kind you are, but I do not wish to join your party, Lord Roxbury." She enunciated each word with care. "Nor will I allow my charge to dash off on such a harebrained excursion with a stranger."

Lady Isabel appeared ready to faint. "You forget yourself, Mrs. Sample. It is not customary . . . you simply cannot . . ."

Caroline turned to Lord Roxbury, her firmly indented Hearn chin lifted. "Thank you for your kind suggestion, sir, but I find that I do not wish to leave London after all."

Lord Roxbury sketched a cool bow and departed. A group of ladies surrounded Lady Isabel, and Dillon caught their censorious glances, which they did not bother to conceal, as they commiserated with her hostess. "What must Roxbury think of us, for after all we are distant cousins!" Lady Isabel mourned.

Lord Roxbury took his departure after another dance with Arabella. Caroline did not lack for partners, Dillon observed with satisfaction, whatever Lady Isabel and Roxbury thought of her background.

On the way home in the carriage the three women were alone, Mortimer having slipped off to some late night activity of his own.

"I cannot think what came over you, Mrs. Sample," Lady Isabel said over and over. "To insult one of our great peers—it was unthinkable in you. If my girls' governess had behaved in such a ramshackle fashion, I should have sent her packing at once, I assure you!"

To which Caroline snapped, "Mrs. Sample is not a servant, Lady Isabel. She is my dear friend and confidante. I will not have *her* insulted, either!"

"I did not mean it quite as I spoke," Lady Isabel mumbled. "We will forget the matter. Though Botham Abbey is considered beautiful and I have never been invited there before," she added wistfully.

Dillon lay awake in the damp, small hours listening to the rain and trying to plot a course of action to prevent her beloved niece from falling into an infatuation with Lord Roxbury.

For she knew how dangerous he was. Call him Lord Roxbury, but never forget that he is really Charles Norton, despite the scar and his hair the years had turned dark, despite his dandyish airs and his preoccupation with his own importance: no one who had been kissed by him could forget the curve of that expressive, full-lipped mouth or the timbre of his deep voice. Nor the electric vitality he generated within himself that belied his deliberate motions. He was more alive than any other man she had ever known.

And how she despised him! Her body tingled with it, as it had once quivered with love.

She had not been entirely sure, however, until she had asked Lady Isabel one final question.

"His given name? Charles Norton. His eldest brother was George, after the father, and the second son was Philip. What a dreadful tragedy it was. The father and two sons drowned on their way back from Ireland, leaving only Charles to inherit. It was several years before he was found to claim his estates, for he had married and lived in Jamaica."

So it was undoubtedly Charles Norton, the man who had sworn to love Dillon Hearn forever, who had never bothered to meet her in the park but had instead sailed to the Caribbean and found a wealthy widow to marry there. She could not be mistaken about him now.

Had he recognized her in her guise of Mrs. Matilda Sample? Having searched his handsome face for some sign of recollection, if not of shame or regret, Dillon found nothing at all there.

It was true that she had changed a great deal. She was nothing like the lighthearted girl he had known. He too had changed, his face carved into rugged lines, his personality congealed into weary cynicism, his impulsive ways now stiff and regimented, yet she knew him.

It was morning before Dillon slept. She shed some tears for the end of a dream shared by two young people who had, one way or another, betrayed themselves and each other.

Somehow I never dreamed that I would grow so old and plain he would not even recognize my face, she thought before she fell asleep. Still, what he thinks of *me* does not matter. I must do my possible to save Caroline from him now.

CHAPTER THREE

Dillon fired her opening gun the following morning at breakfast, which Emerald served to her and Caroline in Caroline's room, much the larger and better furnished of the two bedrooms.

"It was clever of you to give Lord Roxbury the setdown he deserved at Almack's last night," she praised, even as she poked distastefully at an object she thought must be a kidney. "From the gossip I have heard, not even the Regent is so impressed with his own consequence as my Lord Roxbury."

Her lovely face turned away toward the fire, Caroline said thoughtfully, "Lord Roxbury has a right to be proud, Aunt Dilly. He is one of the first peers of the realm, the owner of vast estates, and an intelligent, handsome, brave gentleman as well."

Dillon's temper caught fire. "Does that give him the right to insult visitors to his country? True, I am of no importance in his scheme of things, but I believe the only true gentleman is one who treats even the least persons with kindliness."

"He did not mean to hurt you, I'm sure." Caroline appeared distressed. "You spoke rather brusquely, and he is unused to that. I hope you will learn to endure him, at the least, because I cannot give up my friendship with Arabella, and therefore we must sometimes be in the same company with Lord Roxbury. You need show only formal politeness, nothing more."

"Let us not delude ourselves, Caroline. Lord Roxbury is by way of becoming your suiter. I believe your parents will never accept such a match."

"On the contrary! He is everything Mama could wish for me. His title and estates are beyond exception."

"He is far too old for you. What has he accomplished beyond marriage to a wealthy widow and falling heir to an estate by accident?"

"Arabella says he won great honor at Trafalgar when he was a young man. And," said Caroline, her strong Hearn chin set, "I find him delightful company."

"So is every man who woos a young, impressionable girl. Only imagine the consequences if you lost your head and married him! You are not too young to realize that he is notorious for his amours. Once the honeymoon ended you would find yourself stowed away in his dank Abbey with his unpleasant stepson while my lord pursued his pleasures elsewhere!"

"Arabella tells me that Juan is a dear boy, only thirteen and quite shy." Caroline's smile was mischievous. "And I trust that I could keep Lord Roxbury's affections engaged beyond the honeymoon, if I were to marry him. Such a notion is premature. I shall be seeing little of him until the night of the ball he gives for Arabella, for he is gone to Paris."

Lulled by this fortunate news, Dillon said, "The ball? Oh, I remember Lady Isabel mentioning it. We will simply pretend to some illness and send our regrets. I have no desire to accept his hospitality."

Caroline's cup clattered into its saucer. "But Roxbury's ball for Arabella is to be the most famous affair of the Season! I can't bear to miss it. Arabella would never forgive me."

"I can tie up my jaw and claim a toothache. You can say that you dare not leave me alone."

"I'm shocked at your duplicity, Aunt Dilly. You always taught me to value truth above everything."

"Remember the old quotation that suggests one do as the Romans when in Rome? Truth is of as little use, here in London during the Season, as a pocket full of Indian wampum. Since prevarication is the mode, I am willing to prevaricate."

"You may fib all you wish, but it won't serve, Aunt Dill! Lady Isabel will be delighted to chaperone me. In fact, she'll be glad of your absence."

"True. Very true." Dillon pushed at her topheavy mass of hair, which refused to stay in place beneath one of Matilda Sample's frilled nightcaps. She sat up straight and put aside her plate. "I shall attend the ball if for no other reason than to keep Lady Isabel out of countenance. Show me the gown you plan to wear."

Emerald ran to fetch a confection of blue and gold lace-trimmed sarsenet. Caroline held it up before herself while Dillon regarded her critically.

"Insipid," Dillon pronounced. "Emerald, did I hear you say Madame Fleur is the best dressmaker

38

in London? Send off a message asking her to consult with us tomorrow." She leaned back and poured more chocolate into her cup. "How long do we have to prepare? Less than three weeks? We'll manage. If we must attend Roxbury's ball, then I intend to go in style."

On the night of the Roxbury ball, Lord and Lady Neville and Mortimer were dressed and waiting, and the carriage had already been brought around before Caroline finally made her appearance.

Caroline floated down the stairs, exquisite in peach-bloom illusion over satin the precise shade of her thick, gold hair, which Emile had piled into a high chignon entwined with live peach blossoms. Mortimer, his puffy face bedazzled, hurried forward to take her arm.

At the foot of the staircase he came to a sudden halt and stared upward, his mouth open in amazement.

"Mrs. Sample! Deuced if I didn't think you was a stranger! Hardly recognized you in that getup!"

Lord Neville stirred in his chair and opened one eye, after which he gave a grunt of surprise. "Dashed fine looking costume, Mrs. Sample. Beats those puckery gowns you was used to wear. Never knew you was such a fine figure of a woman."

"What have you done to your hair?" Lady Isabel cried out in horror. "Mrs. Sample, where is your widow's cap!"

Dillon descended the last few steps with an air of confidence.

"I have discarded the caps as being unnecessary and uncomfortable, Lady Isabel. It was impossible to keep them firmly attached to my hair, which was ever unmanageable, until Emile decided to cut it in this short, simple style, which makes it wonderfully easy to keep."

"Your gown?" Lady Isabel appeared about to faint. "So—so clinging . . ."

Caroline spoke up before Dillon could reply.

"I think it is most becoming, Lady Isabel. Mrs. Sample is still young, and there is no reason for her to dress in widows' weeds forever. After all, she lost her husband some ten years ago."

"Handsome woman, now that she's got up in the mode," Lord Neville contributed. He lurched to his feet and offered Dillon his arm, though in the end it was she who supported him to the carriage.

Long before they reached Roxbury House, they found themselves caught in a great crush of vehicles all bound in the same direction.

"We will be among the last to arrive," Lady Neville kept on lamenting as they inched forward toward the tall, lighted facade of the imposing stone pile.

That she was right Dillon was forced to admit to herself as they climbed the grand staircase, saw the crowded rooms, and heard the subdued but powerful roar of conversation among the assembled guests. As she awaited her turn to greet her host and his niece, Dillon felt a flutter of nervousness until she took note of a faintly musty odor emanating from the velvet draperies. Hah, she thought. And no doubt there are mice in the lower regions! They are not so grand as they believe, after all.

She advanced along the reception line toward her

host, who stood flanked by Arabella and Mrs. Worthing, as well as by her sister and her husband, Lord Pomfret. Charles Norton bowed and smiled with an air of cool indifference that made Dillon long to put him in his place. As if we are all so humble we should give thanks to be invited here, she fumed inwardly!

"Lord and Lady Neville, Sir Mortimer Neville, Miss Caroline Hearn, Mrs. Sample," the butler intoned.

The rigid correctness of Roxbury's features only altered when Caroline greeted him with her serene smile. "We can begin now that you are arrived," he said, bending over her gloved hand. "Arabella has been frantic with worry that you were ill. How beautiful you look tonight. You and Arabella should certainly sweep the lists, as you put it."

He passed Caroline along with some reluctance to a bubbling Arabella, who was as charming as a French Doll in pink with pink ribbons in her dark hair, and he turned to Dillon. For a fearful moment he stared at her in surprise, which he took no trouble to conceal.

Dillon sketched a bow and passed on to be welcomed by Arabella and her mother, Mrs. Worthing. Her pulse pounded with angry triumph. He had recognized her, she thought. He must know now that he could not trifle with Caroline's affections without being checkmated by her, who had it in her power to inform her niece of his habit of infidelity.

Crowded as the ballroom was, a slight hush fell over the guests when Caroline entered, followed by Dillon. Of course they were all admiring Caroline, Dillon thought proudly, until she realized that she, too, was the object of many covert glances. Let them stare! It was amazing how much confidence one gained from being well dressed.

Until her meeting with Madame Fleur, Dillon had dismissed fashion as a matter of ruffles and furbelows. "Which I cannot abide!" she had told the French modiste firmly.

Madame Fleur had thrown out her hands expressively. "*Mais non!* Rid yourself of that hideous garment you wear and we shall see!"

In a cozy, gray velvet dressing room, Dillon felt that she was shedding the character of prosy Matilda Sample along with her ugly lavender gown. She turned, bent, and let herself be measured while Madame Fleur began to smile.

"What a game we shall make of the widow's colors, eh? So proper and demure in white or gray or black, but cut to show off the fine shape and bring out the rose complexion."

Her ball gown was so plain as to make all the others look overdone. Of the finest white satin, it was cut with the high Empire waistline and slim skirt, its low décolletage banded demurely with narrow strips of black velvet ribbon that matched the bands at the hem of her skirt. A silvery shawl draped lightly from her shoulders, and she wore the pearls her father had given her on her twenty-first birthday.

As she took a chair beside Arabella's mother, that lady said kindly, "You are very young to be left a widow, my dear. And with no children to live for! My own four are all my life. You must come for a visit and let me show you the other three. Oh, do look. The dancing is about to begin. Charles is leading off with my Arabella. There is Caroline with her cousin Mortimer. Is it true that she has a *tendre* for him? Arabella says not."

"I hope not, I assure you, Mrs. Worthing!"

The plump little woman leaned closer to Dillon and whispered, "Arabella looks for a match between her dear Uncle Charles and your Caroline. She is a beautiful child. No wonder Charles cannot take his eyes from her."

"Such a match would not please her family. They would not want her to live across the ocean from home."

Mrs. Worthing opened her round, brown eyes wide. "But my dear Mrs. Sample, Roxbury is the greatest catch in England!"

"There are families in America who own properties even larger than Roxbury's. Caroline might marry any one of their sons who are close to her in age."

Kind Mrs. Worthing hesitated, obviously careful not to hurt the feelings of her foreign friend. "But— money only? None of the young men you speak of can compare with Roxbury in birth, I believe, and that is so important. My Arabella, I must confide, is infatuated with Sir John Huddleston, whose title is not an old one and who has only a modest property. I dare not forbid Sir John the house for fear she might take it into her head to run off with him, but I am doing all in my power to discourage the affair."

A dozen retorts flamed in Dillon's head, but she was as careful as Mrs. Worthing to avoid offense. "I believe that a man's character matters more than his birth or his property. If Caroline should fall in love with a decent young man who happened to be poor but honorable, her parents would accept the match."

"But at eighteen our girls are in and out of love so quickly, it is important to give them time."

Before Dillon could reply, Mrs. Worthing noticed the approach of Lady Isabel and smiled a welcome. Lady Isabel did not return her smile. Her wrinkled face tight with disapprobation, she led forward a gentleman with a round, reddish face who, though properly dressed in knee breeches and velvet coat, bore a vaguely disheveled appearance.

"Mrs. Sample," said Lady Isabel, "I am come to present Mr. Forster to you. He is a member of Lord Roxbury's household."

"Tutor to young Juan," Mr. Forster interrupted. "Miss Hearn tells me that you have an interest in my own hobby. Books, my dear lady! If I may have the next dance, I should like to tell you about certain priceless acquisitions I have recently made to add to Lord Roxbury's library."

Dillon regarded him with complete surprise. "At my age, in my position, it would be unseemly to dance."

"Oh, come. There can be nothing improper in your enjoyment of a simple country dance. Caroline says you have been a widow for many years. You cannot wear weeds forever."

Dillon's feet, in her morocco slippers, had been keeping time to the music ever since she had sat down in her gilt chair. How long it had been since she had danced! She stood up recklessly. Tonight she had broken so many rules that breaking one more could hardly matter. She put her hand on the jolly tutor's arm and took her place on the floor when the set formed.

Across from them, Lord Roxbury led his partner forward. She was a tall, handsome blonde, with large features and prominent blue eyes, who clung to Roxbury's arm and whispered something to him that caused him to glance across at Dillon and the tutor with a faint smile.

Dillon lifted her tilted nose somewhat higher. "Who is the ill-mannered female staring at us?" she inquired, not troubling to keep her voice low.

Mr. Forster blushed redly, sketching a bow toward his employer.

"It is the Countess of Demford, a famed beauty," he murmured under cover of the music as the musicians struck up.

"One of Lord Roxbury's flirts, no doubt. Do please point out her husband to me, Mr. Forster. No, wait. Let me see if I can guess which one he is."

"How will you go about discovering him in this crush?" the tutor inquired, stepping on her toe as they circled.

"I shall look for a man who is elderly, probably ill or crippled with the gout. He will be sitting with cronies in his same circumstances, but his eyes will be following his young wife."

"You are either a witch or you are roasting me, Mrs. Sample. That is the earl sitting in the alcove with his gouty foot up on a stool."

Dillon saw that the earl was in his sixties, if not older. He was handsome for his age, poor man. But she had no more time to spare for him, her feet having responded joyously to the music from the first note. She had forgotten how enjoyable it was to dance. Once or twice she reached up in an automatic gesture to straighten her hair, only to smile in secret delight when she touched her newly shorn locks and found them rioting with curl in the heat of the ballroom. It was all such fun that she forgave poor Mr. Forster for his clumsiness.

When that gentleman returned Dillon to Lady Isabel, much to that lady's disapproval, he begged her for a waltz later in the evening. "For you are a wonderfully accomplished dancer, Mrs. Sample, and I am not fully familiar with the dance as yet."

After Dillon had accepted and he had gone away, Lady Isabel said coldly, "Surely you will not dance the waltz, madam. One simple country dance may be forgiven, but there is bound to be criticism if you flaunt yourself."

"It is hardly flaunting to enjoy a simple pleasure."

"You are a widow! It is not decent for you to appear to enjoy yourself, especially with a gentleman."

Dillon called Lady Isabel's attention to the countess, who was engaged in a flirtatious passage with Lord Roxbury. "If it is acceptable for a married woman to behave so, why may I not tread a decorous measure with Mr. Forster?"

Her hostess made it plain that Dillon's ignorance wearied her.

"Once a woman marries and provides an heir, she is free to do as she pleases, depending upon her husband's moods. Besides which, the countess is related to the royal family."

I see, thought Dillon, her eyes alight with mischief. What's common in a commoner is commonplace among the aristocracy. And who cares? Not I. Her feet danced under her satin skirt, and her eyes roamed over the thronged ballroom, gathering impressions she meant to store away in her travel diary before she slept that night. Unaware of the lively picture she made, she scarcely noticed when, in the next interval, a stocky gentleman whose large square head was covered with gray curls approached and spoke to Lady Isabel.

He had already bowed over the lady's hand and murmured some polite inquiries as to her health when Dillon heard him say, "I beg you will present me to your companion, Lady Neville."

"To my comp—to Mrs. Sample, Your Grace?" Lady Isabel faltered. "Are you sure you wish to . . . ?"

"I saw her during the reel and made sure I must have a dance with the lady. Mrs. Sample, if that is your name, I congratulate you on your light feet. Why have I not met you before?"

"Because I am only a visitor in London."

"May I present the Duke of Burnley?" Lady Isabel said in a faint voice. "This lady is chaperone to Miss Caroline Hearn, our cousin from the States."

"A Colonial!" The duke was set back but recovered to ask, "Have you left your husband at home or in the card room, madam?"

"It was he who left me for a better world many years ago, Your Grace. I am a widow."

The duke cast another appraising glance over Dillon's face and figure and appeared pleased with what he saw.

"You must have married out of the schoolroom,

Mrs. Sample. The set is forming for the lancers. May I?"

She stood up and put her hand on his arm, aware of the curious eyes that followed their progress. Like a gale wind, whispers rose to a crescendo throughout the room. Dillon caught a glimpse of Caroline looking in her direction with raised eyebrows as the girl took her place with Mortimer.

"Demmed beauty," the duke remarked, having noted the direction of Dillon's glance.

"She is my—er—my responsibility while we are in London. Miss Caroline Hearn."

"Ah, of course. The American they say Roxbury will offer for. A big dowry, I understand, not that it signifies since Roxbury is already sinfully in pocket. Lucky fellow," the duke said enviously.

The duke danced with some grace, unlike Mr. Forster, but Dillon was disconcerted to find that whenever they met in the intricacies of the figure, he gave her waist an intimate squeeze. Foreign customs notwithstanding, Dillon spoke up after the third attack.

"That was rather painful, Your Grace. Be kind enough to hold me lightly next time. You do not realize your own strength."

She raised her eyes innocently and smiled. The duke's weathered face reddened. She half expected that he would lead her back to Lady Isabel like a naughty child to her nurse. Then, unexpectedly, he gave her a lopsided smile in return.

"You have spirit, Mrs. Sample. You remind me of my mama, though you are much younger, of course."

The set was coming to an end when the duke panted in her ear, "Do you ride, Mrs. Sample?"

"Of course I do."

They were swept apart and met again only as the music ended. The duke led Dillon back slowly to the frail shelter of Lady Isabel, talking all the way. "We must get up a party and visit Benwell Castle soon. You will want to see our Roman ruins and of course the Castle."

"You are kind, Your Grace, but I think we will be returning to America very soon."

The duke began to describe the Castle and his Roman ruins in persuasive tones and had only started on the Norman tower when they were interrupted by an amused masculine voice from behind them.

"You waste your time if you expect to coax Mrs. Sample into a visit to the country, Burnley. I have tried and failed."

Dillon halted and took a calming breath before she turned and bestowed a syrupy smile upon Lord Roxbury, who had Caroline on one arm and Arabella on the other.

"But you did not offer me a Norman tower, Lord Roxbury," she said, "nor any Roman ruins. I vow, I cannot allow Miss Hearn to leave England without having seen something of its history."

The duke was not slow to pick up the glove. "Three weeks from tonight, shall we say, Lady Isabel? A small party, no more than twelve. I can't abide crowds, you know. You will have to come with Miss Hearn, Roxbury."

"I should like nothing better," Lord Roxbury drawled, "but that happens to be the weekend of the Tiger's mill with two contenders, which means I am already engaged."

"Too bad," the duke said cheerfully. "We shan't have any trouble finding another partner for Miss Hearn. Lady Isabel, my mother will be in touch with you. Your servant." He bowed to Dillon and was seen to make his way across the crowded room toward the countess, who sat pouting beside her gouty husband.

"What an unusual person," Caroline said, staring at his retreating back.

"He was a friend of the King, you know, before his mind . . . But that is all past, and Benwell is one of our greatest estates . . . and he wishes me to make arrangements with the dowager . . ." Lady Isabel knotted her twiglike fingers in an agony of delight.

"He is an intolerable old lecher," Roxbury interrupted.

"Is that something out of the way? I had believed it to be the custom among English peers," Dillon remarked with an air of innocence.

Roxbury looked down at her, and their eyes met and locked. Now he is *sure* he knows me, Dillon thought in painful triumph. He must realize that I have forgotten nothing and that I will oppose him at every stage if he attempts to hurt Caroline as he hurt me.

After an uncomfortable silence, Roxbury shrugged.

"You are not a green girl, Mrs. Sample, so perhaps I need warn you no further. However, you should know that the duke has married and buried two wives and cast aside innumerable—ladies who imagined he was deeply attached to them. He has vowed not to marry again."

"In that case we will get on together famously. Oh, Mr. Forster. Is this our waltz? How delightful." She sailed away on the tutor's arm, while Roxbury led Caroline out and Sir John Huddleston arrived to claim another dance with Arabella.

The ballroom turned into a giddy kaleidoscope of couples revolving in the new German dance under shimmering crystal chandeliers. The room was so crowded that after two near collisions, Lord Roxbury guided Caroline toward the open French windows, where islands of potted palms formed niches of comparative calm. As they glided around their sheltered corner, Caroline heard a familiar voice through the hedge of palm leaves.

"If you will only take smaller steps, Mr. Forster, we will deal together much better. Oh, excellent! You are coming on to the waltz nicely."

"Thank you," the tutor panted. "May I suggest that you allow me to lead? In our country it is the custom."

"I am sorry! Teaching my boys to dance has left me in the habit of leading, I fear."

"How many boys do you have, Mrs.Sample?"

"I'm not quite sure. It varies from year to year. Perhaps twenty at present."

"Yet you appear to be so youthful!"

A moment later Caroline heard the tutor apologize. Plainly he had been so disconcerted that he had missed his step. She bit her lips in order to stave off a childish fit of the giggles.

Roxbury murmured into Caroline's ear suavely, "With so many, one cannot expect Mrs. Sample to

51

recall the exact count. If one added in daughters, of whom there must be a few, no mama, however, doting, could be expected to keep the numbers straight."

"I forbid you to roast me about my beloved Mrs. Sample, sir. She has no children. Mr. Sample died very soon after they were married."

A gleam lighted Roxbury's dark blue eyes. "You need say no more. I understand. Imagining that he had wed a sweet, tractable girl, he soon discovered that his wife meant to govern him in every way, including the waltz and he promptly gave up the ghost."

Caroline craned over Roxbury's elegantly tailored shoulder and saw that Aunt Dilly was indeed leading Mr. Forster again. She must warn her about the bad habit when they were alone.

"Mr. Sample was thrown from his horse and killed," she explained repressively. "As for her boys, Mrs. Sample is a famous scholar. Her pupils at the Latin School will miss her profoundly."

"She and Forster should find a great deal in common."

"So I believe. I am already matchmaking."

Spying an opening in the throng, Lord Roxbury moved Caroline out and away from their leafy bower.

"Forster is wellborn but has no expectations."

"That would not matter to my—to Mrs. Sample. She has property of her own. But now that I have introduced them, I am of two minds. If they married, I could not bear to have her living across an ocean from me."

Lord Roxbury slowed his step and looked down

into Caroline's lovely flushed face with an intent expression. "You might settle in England yourself. Have you considered that possibility?"

Caroline lowered her lashes. "No, I have not."

"But you will?" he pressed.

"Perhaps. I am still a stranger to your ways."

Smiling as if satisfied with her reply, Roxbury swung Caroline in a last extravagant whirl before he released her and returned her to the custody of Lady Isabel, who sat nodding in her stiff chair.

"Since you have given away all remaining dances, I must bid you good night," he said to her softly. "Miss Hearn, would you have me forgo the boxing match and accompany you to Benwell Castle? My fate is in your hands."

"You exaggerate, Lord Roxbury. You must choose your own fate."

He bowed, smiling, and took his leave. Caroline, seating herself in the chair next to her hostess, leaned toward Lady Isabel with an expression of concern.

"Are you feeling perfectly well, Lady Neville?"

"I shall be better when I am in bed," that lady replied querulously. "What has become of Mrs. Sample? Really, what people are saying about her! I did not expect I should have to serve as chaperone to her as well as to you, dear child. It is all most unnerving."

Rain dripped with a solemn regularity outside Caroline's window next morning as she and her aunt broke their fasts together. Not even the lively fire Emerald had kindled could banish the ancient chill of Neville House on a gray May morning.

Caroline sat cross-legged on the rug before the fire, while Dillon kept restlessly busy examining the floral offerings sent to Caroline by her admirers.

"Roses from Alsonett again," Caroline remarked, biting into a piece of Emerald's soda bread with enjoyment. "He is a dear but such a lightweight! The posy of violets came from Dalrymple. He writes that the color matches my eyes. A poem came with the posy but I burnt it for fear you would laugh. Emerald, what in heaven's name is that?"

The maid came in bearing an enormous basket filled to overflowing with hothouse fruits nestled amid branches of greenery and blossom.

" 'Tis from the Duke of Burnley for Miss Dillon," Emerald announced in mournful tones.

"Aunt Dill, you've made a famous conquest! Lord Roxbury is small potatoes in comparison. May I have a peach?"

"Take what you like. You too, Emerald. I shall try the green grapes. Emerald, don't stand there staring. Come closer to the fire. Your hands are positively blue. Don't they keep a proper fire below stairs?"

"Only for their own, Miss Dillon. They don't like me to edge in for fear I'll hear them gossip. This morning they were saying that Miss Caroline is to marry the lord with the scar on his proud face!" Emerald sank down on the hearth rug and burst into tears. "Now there's a duke after you, Miss Dillon! And me breaking my heart to go home to America and yet not if I have to leave either of you in this benighted land without me."

"I have no intention of marrying anyone, much less a duke," Dillon assured her warmly.

Caroline meanwhile bit into her peach, dabbing at her chin ineffectually when the juice began to run. "Delicious! But you will have to decide for yourself whether it is worth while to marry Burnley for fresh peaches and green grapes. As for me, I have not made up my mind yet. Perhaps I would like being the lady of Botham Abbey."

Dillon put down her grapes in dismay. "I never thought you would lose your head over a title!"

Caroline threw her aunt a wicked grin. "I would be in more danger if a *duke* offered for me."

Face flaming, Dillon bent over the basket and pretended to examine the lavish display inside. "A pineapple—how exotic. My boys would go into ecstasies although they would first blunt their teeth trying to get through the skin." She straightened up with a daffodil in her hands and said with an air of resolution, "It is near time for your admirers to come calling, Caroline. We had better hurry with our dress. Lady Isabel sent word that she expects me to play hostess since she is unwell today."

Some little time later, Dillon, having greeted near a dozen young gentlemen who hovered around Caroline eagerly, made up her mind that there was safety in numbers. The thought had scarcely taken form before Petman, the butler, who maintained an air of haughty disdain except when he was satisfied with the quality of the visitor, announced in ringing tones, "Lord Roxbury."

That gentleman advanced into the room with cool aplomb, his exquisitely fitted coat and gleaming Hessians putting to shame the extravagances of the younger men who scattered before him like cubs before a lion, Dillon noticed. Caroline's face glowed as she welcomed him and thanked him for his bouquet of tiny golden roses which, she told him, she had chosen to carry to the rout at Lady Almendingen's that evening.

"Then I regret even more deeply that I cannot be present to see my flowers in your hands, Miss Hearn. I have been called home to Botham Abbey. My stepson is unwell."

"I hope it is nothing serious."

"Juan is subject to mysterious fevers. It is difficult to be sure this is not another false alarm, but I am determined to see for myself."

"Of course you must, but Arabella will miss you."

"And so will Miss Hearn, I hope. Without my awesome presence to restrain your legion of admirers, your morning rides in the Park are sure to resemble a convocation of the troops."

Caroline laughed. "I had not considered it, but what fun! Bella and I will drill our troops as rigorously as the great Duke of Wellington. Squads to the right, to the left, and forward march! Am I doing it properly?"

Roxbury's eyes rested on her face, and a faint smile moved over his composed features. "I would obey you on the instant."

Caroline's composure slipped for a moment. "Have you seen Arabella today? I half expected her to call."

"She was just leaving for a walk in the Park with John Huddleston when I stopped to pay my compliments."

"A walk in the rain?" Dillon inquired doubtfully.

"Arabella has spent most of her life in the country, Mrs. Sample," Roxbury replied condescendingly. "Rain means nothing to her."

He turned back to address Caroline. Dillon caught an exchange of intimate glances between them. But she must take care not to fall into a pucker, she warned herself. It was fortunate that Roxbury had been called back to his abbey. In his absence there would be time to bend Caroline in the direction of some more attractive and younger gallant.

Alsonett? Lighthearted, handsome, reckless, yet Dillon feared he was not the kind to match up against one of Roxbury's consequence. There was Taverner, who stood to inherit an earldom one day, but he was a pompous bore who talked on and on in a dry monotone about his prowess in the hunt. Caroline could endure anything but a husband who was a bore. Canham was openly bowled over by Caroline's beauty, but it was common knowledge (according to Emerald) that he was in deep water financially.

Preoccupied as she was by her anxious thoughts as well as the tangle of knots she had made of the purse she was supposed to be netting, Dillon did not realize that Roxbury had taken the chair beside hers until she heard him say in his hatefully suave voice, "I trust you were not overly fatigued by last night's excitements, Mrs. Sample."

"I am not so decrepit that a little dancing exhausts me."

"You and your good husband were accustomed to attend a great many social functions, I imagine?"

"We enjoyed dancing." Dillon closed her lips

quickly. It was not quite an untruth. Roxbury need not know that she meant her boys when she said "we."

In her agitation she had dropped her web of knots. Roxbury picked it up and returned it to her courteously, though not before he gave it a long, amused scrutiny.

"Your husband was a planter, I believe? I seem to have heard of a Sample who grew first-rate tobacco leaf."

Dillon bent over her knots in panic. What in heaven's name had Henry Sample done? She hoped she appeared suitably dismal as she replied, "Forgive me, but I prefer not to speak of Mr. Sample. Oh, here is young Mr. Taverner waiting to speak to me. You will excuse me?"

Roxbury rose, sketched a bow, and made his way slowly toward the door. He had not quite reached his goal when the door opened and Petman announced almost under his breath, "Mr. Forster." Roxbury halted in surprise.

"You haven't had my message?" he inquired of the tutor as he entered the room. "It's Juan again. We leave for the Abbey in an hour."

Mr. Forster, looking disheveled, sighed. "Señora Mendez grows alarmed every time the boy sneezes. Very well, I'll be at Roxbury House in plenty of time, only first I must present this small gift to Mrs. Sample."

Lord Roxbury gave his son's tutor an odd look before he smiled and took his departure. Caroline's young men, regaining a measure of confidence in Roxbury's absence, commented scornfully when Mrs. Sample opened the gift in question. An old book, no less, sporting a stained binding and worn gilt, when any fellow with sense knew women liked flowers and sweets. To their consternation, Mrs. Sample pounced upon the volume with an uninhibited cry of delight, and Caroline looked at it admiringly.

"I have never seen a Book of Hours quite like this one, Mr. Forster," Mrs. Sample said. "Is it very rare?"

"No, it is only a copy of a much older one. We found quite a dozen of them stored in the attics at the Abbey. It is my hobby to catalogue the many volumes in Lord Roxbury's library. The only reason I have come to London now is to buy up a certain rare bit to add to his collection."

"This is beautiful work, whether or not it is old, and I am grateful to you for giving it to me. It is a shame that your pupil has fallen ill."

"Poor Juan." The tutor's round face turned lugubrious. "He was born and lived in Jamaica during his childhood. As a result, he has never adapted to our English climate."

Hiding a smile, Dillon commented, "That is not really surprising. Is he a good student?"

"Oh, beyond excellence! He spends so much time reading that Charles—Lord Roxbury—and I fear he will damage his frail constitution. We take him out riding whenever Señora Mendez gives her permission, but unfortunately he does not like to hunt."

"Killing is not a sport that appeals to everyone, I believe. It is odd, is it not, that Lord Roxbury does not send the boy to school."

Mr. Forster appeared uncomfortable. "Charles—Lord Roxbury—has no good opinion of Eton or Oxford, I fear. We attended both schools together, you see, since my father has the living at the Abbey, and we grew up almost as brothers. Charles never could abide strict rules. He got into every sort of a scrape a lively boy can manage at Eton, and when we arrived at Oxford, he was sent down almost at once. It was then that his father bought him a commission in the Navy in the belief which my father and I shared that life at sea might suit him. In the event, it did. He performed heroic feats in the war with Napoleon, Mrs. Sample. There is no man I admire more."

Caroline had been listening with eager interest. "Why did he make Jamaica his home, instead of Botham Abbey?"

"Old Lord Roxbury was a martinet, Miss Hearn. He and Charles were ever at swords' point after Charles's mother died. Charles had no reason to want to come home after Trafalgar. He took his small naval award and his injuries to the Caribbean to recuperate in the sun."

"And there met and married a wealthy Spanish woman, I understand," Dillon put in for Caroline's benefit.

Mr. Forster shook his rosy cheeks. "No, no. He had known Mrs. Conynford and her husband when he was only a junior officer, and they had been kind to him. When Conynford died of one of those tropical fevers, Charles did all he could to help his widow and little Juan. Lady Margarita was a very lovely woman, but she was not strong. With her father and her husband dead, she depended upon Charles to manage her estates for her."

"Yes, I see how it might have been," Caroline

murmured sympathetically. "Poor Lord Roxbury. His has not been a particularly happy life."

Before Mr. Forster could relate any more touching stories about Roxbury's past, Dillon rose up and announced that it was time for them to dress if they were to attend Lady Tibbet's afternoon card party. Let Alsonett raise his eyebrows at her abruptness. If she failed to get Caroline away quickly, she and the tutor would be weeping together over "poor Lord Roxbury's unhappy youth!"

At the theater the next evening, Caroline leaned together with her aunt and whispered, "You are in disgrace with Alsonett for your manners, and Taverner is furious because you said King Henry the Eighth plundered the abbeys to enrich himself. Taverner's distant ancestor got his title from King Henry."

"So, I suppose, did Roxbury's family. The Abbey is sure to be haunted by the ghosts of monks who were murdered or sent into exile."

"We may find out when we visit the Abbey," Caroline said mischievously.

Dillon almost dropped her fan. "What do you mean!"

"I have accepted Lord Roxbury's invitation to visit Botham Abbey with Arabella after we leave Benwell Castle. It is only a little out of our way, and we will stay for just two days."

"You will write tomorrow and explain to him that you have changed your mind! Lady Neville would be horrified. Roxbury is an unmarried man of doubtful reputation. Not even my presence would make it proper."

Caroline smiled calmly. "I did not expect it would. Lady Pomfret, his sister, will act as hostess during our visit, so it will be perfectly acceptable to go there."

Dillon spread open her fan, which she carried only for appearance's sake, and began to wave it back and forth so vehemently that Mr. Taverner, sitting behind her, reached up irritably to smooth his carefully arranged locks. Ignoring him, Dillon whispered to her niece, "I fear you have become overly sophisticated since we have come to London."

Caroline reached out to pat her aunt's gloved wrist.

"It doesn't signify, so long as you go on loving me, Aunt Dilly."

CHAPTER FOUR

"A real castle?" Emerald's huge green eyes grew round. "Like in fairy tales?"

They were jolting along in a hired coach on their way to Benwell. Caroline, Dillon, and the maid rode alone, for they were out of favor with the Nevilles since Caroline had refused Mortimer's offer of marriage. Mortimer was presently wooing the daughter of a wealthy nabob only recently returned from India. Invited by the Duke of Burnley to bring along their own party, Lord and Lady Neville had asked Mr. Hornby Daunt and his wife and daughter to share their coach.

The Neville equipage led with way, leaving their hired vehicle to follow behind. Dillon sneezed.

"The Daunts' dust is irritating. So is the Nevilles," she said, fumbling for a kerchief, "although I could breathe Mr. Shakespeare's dust all day and not mind it. Perhaps you should have been gentler about refusing Mortimer, Caroline."

Caroline laughed cheerfully. "I fear Miss Henrietta Daunt has cut me out with him entirely. I have never felt so relieved!"

"If you had felt a *tendre* for Mortimer, I swear I would have disowned you," Dillon said. "Emerald, the castle we are going to visit was built five hundred years ago. It was twice burned and several times ravaged. Some time later, Queen Elizabeth gave it to her favorite courtier. According to rumor, it is haunted by the ghost of that man's wife. She was killed in a fall from a window. Pushed out by her husband, I suspect."

"Now who is the cynic among us?" Caroline protested.

But the day was too lovely to harbor low spirits. With each mile they progressed, the countryside appeared more appealing, lavish with blue and lavender wildflowers along the ditches and whitened by snowdrifts of blooming fruit trees.

"Do you know, I am feeling a little bit homesick," Caroline murmured.

"I too. I wish we were on our way to Hearn Hill."

Dillon's face was sober beneath her fashionable new chip bonnet, for she had been stricken with a sudden sense of foreboding. What with Mortimer paying court to the Daunt female and Arabella and Sir John head over heels, Roxbury was bound to have Caroline to himself while she was kept busy dodging the duke's amorous advances. If only Roxbury had continued to refuse the duke's invitation, as he had done at first! However, it did no good to cry over burnt porridge. Better to think of ways to avert disastrous consequences.

Emerald let down the window as they turned onto a graveled lane and drove smartly along between a row of handsome old beeches. Her red lips rounded into an O. "Never in my life did I see the like of it!

'Tis more beautiful than the King's palace, Miss Dillon. A fairy palace!"

They had driven out of London in a morning mist. Now the sun had emerged through a thin shift of cloud, illuminating the many tall windows of the handsome, sprawling mass of Benwell Castle with a soft golden light so that it did indeed have an enchanted look about it.

As they wheeled behind the Neville coach around a curve toward the massive oaken door, rooks flew up from an ivy-hung tower which was connected to the newer main building by an arched passageway. In every direction smooth greensward stretched into vistas planted with trees and shrubbery of varieties unknown to Dillon, and the shimmer of a small lake beckoned beyond.

"All my mama's doing," the duke explained after the party had been welcomed and introduced to the dowager duchess, a tiny woman with a hint of red in curls not quite concealed beneath her cap. "Sad ruin this place was when I inherited."

"Sheep on the terrace," the dowager agreed, "and no drains to speak of." She directed her bright blue gaze toward Dillon. "*You* will understand, I am sure. You have a sensible air. Ah, Lady Neville. So this is your Mortimer."

She stared in polite disbelief at his tight coat and striped vest cluttered with fobs. Lady Neville hastened to bring forward the Daunts with a little speech about their interesting Indian background. The dowager listened, nodded, and then appeared to dismiss them from her consciousness.

"Mrs. Sample, come and let me show you how I

have arranged to bring warm water into the kitchens. You are certain to be pleased."

It was not until later, after the party had partaken of a hearty lunch, that Caroline and Dillon found time to share their initial impressions. Assigned to adjoining rooms at Benwell, as they were at Neville House, this time it was Dillon who lodged in the choice apartment. Caroline smiled inwardly as she came through their shared dressing room to join her aunt. She took a seat near the hearth and looked down with an odd expression at Dillon, who pretended to poke at a small fire.

"Don't plague me, I beg," Dillon muttered hurriedly.

"Of course I shan't. I was only wondering whether I must address you as Your Grace when you are mistress of Benwell. I hope you will allow me to dispense with a curtsy when we are alone together."

"How many times must I tell you that I have no intention of marrying!" Dillon sat back on her heels, and her hot look changed. "Though Benwell is indeed beautiful enough to tempt a weaker woman. At any rate, I do not believe the duke's intentions are honorable, whatever his mother may assume."

"The dowager is a dear. You're rather like her, Aunt Dill. The duke beamed on both of you equally."

"I have no notion of playing mama to him or any man. Now may we please talk of some other subject?"

Emerald knocked and came in to collect their gowns to be pressed, bringing word that Lord Roxbury had arrived in a curricle with match grays fine enough to knock your eye out.

"He's got that groom O'Toole with him, him one of the black Irish with a mouth full of white teeth and always smiling."

"At you?" Caroline inquired.

Emerald flushed a glorious pink. "Among others! They're all after him, even that sour old dresser of Lady Neville's. Lord Neville is foxed already, and Mortimer has gone walking in the shrubbery with the elephant—I'm sorry, Miss Dillon—I mean with Miss Daunt. Miss Arabella and Sir John are down by the lake. The duke's gone to show Lord Roxbury his stables. His mama, the dowager, asked me to tell Mrs. Sample that she wishes to talk to her in the solarium before tea."

Dillon jumped up in a fluster. "Tell her that I can't leave Caroline unchaperoned."

"I have already engaged to meet Arabella and Sir John at the lake, Aunt Dilly. I'm perfectly willing to play gooseberry with them while you and your future mama-in-law discuss the castle drains."

Dillon glanced around the room like a hunted creature. "I—I believe I have a headache coming on."

"It won't do, Aunt Dill, not when you look in such blooming health. Nor when the dowager is such a dear. You cannot offend her."

"What if she wants to know how I feel about her son?"

"Tell her the truth. Say you hardly know him and are not inclined to marry again. That way you'll gain time to think it over."

67

"I don't need time. I like the duke, and his attentions are flattering, but I cannot love him."

"Liking often grows into something deeper, Aunt Dilly. Give yourself time."

"You take Miss Caroline's advice," urged Emerald as she went toward the door carrying piles of muslin and silk and satin over her arms. "She was born knowing more about how to handle the gentlemen than most females learn in a lifetime. I heard a lady say that one night at Hearn Hill."

"While I am as innocent as a newborn babe in such arts?" Dillon inquired acidly. Maid and niece stared at her in amazement. She gave them a sheepish grin. "Oh, pay no attention to my tempers. How I wish we were safe at home in Philadelphia! This frivolous way of life does not suit me."

After she had rested and bathed, Dillon chose her favorite new gown from Madame Fleur, of fine muslin cut severely with a narrow skirt that showed off to advantage her slight but shapely figure, although she was unaware of that fact, having chosen it for its simplicity and comfort and because she liked its lilac color, which Madame Fleur had spiced adroitly with bands of deep green grosgrain while eschewing frills completely.

She dismissed Emerald after her bath. Alone, she brushed her cropped curls vigorously, stepped into delicate morocco slippers, and was ready.

Not without a qualm, she made her way to the solarium some fifteen minutes before tea was to be served. Enough time, she trusted, to fulfill the dowager's request for a private talk, yet less than the dowager might desire if she meant to probe deeply into Dillon's emotional state.

Shown in by Herblock, the rotund butler who appeared to approve of her, she found the dowager on her feet dusting an ugly porcelain figurine with her handkerchief.

"Shepherdesses were all the thing in the old days," that lady remarked briskly as she replaced the piece on a table. "Marie Antoinette started the fad. She loved laying the rustic, no doubt in reaction to the pomp and ceremony she endured all her life. Poor Marie—she wasn't evil, she was simply a pawn in the game of kings."

The dowager beckoned Dillon to a seat next to her on a cushioned settee. She looked her guest over frankly and smiled.

"That is a very handsome gown, Mrs. Sample. Madame Fleur, I imagine. I take it that your husband left you well placed?"

"I am comfortable, yes. My investments have done well."

"You understand such matters?"

Dillon shifted as if to escape from the net of untruth in which she was becoming entangled.

"I'm afraid I do. I have always been good at figures."

"Admirable! So have I. It is strange that a woman of your beauty has not married again."

Dillon's surprise showed plainly. "Why, I am nothing like a beauty, Your Grace!"

"Perhaps not according to the insipid mode that prevails, but you have a certain spirit that lends character to your presence. I find it difficult to believe that you have not been sought in marriage since your husband's death."

"I let it be known that I am perfectly content with my life as it is."

The dowager's lips curved slightly. "I am sure you are not the sort to lead a man on. How sad that you were left alone at such a young age, with no children to comfort you." The dowager's slender face, which was still lovely, misted softly, and she looked younger than her years. "I have three daughters and a dozen grandchildren. It is only my son who worries me. What a misfortune that both his wives died young. And—to be frank with you, dear child—that they were pretty little creatures with no strength of character at all. Randolph needs a strong woman to order his estates."

"The duke has two grown sons to inherit," Dillon pointed out uneasily. "Surely, with the succession assured, he need not marry again."

The dowager put her hand lightly on Dillon's wrist. "I'm not young. I can't protect him forever from light-skirts and cheating tradesmen and mamas whose silly little daughters long to capture a duke. I am delighted beyond measure that Randolph has finally got the wit to appreciate a woman who will suit him. Perhaps he is growing up at last! Randolph is exceedingly lovable, Mrs. Sample. Careless sometimes, and undependable, but a sweet, affectionate boy at heart."

"I—I hardly know the duke. We danced one evening, and he paid us a call at Neville House."

"He would not have invited you here to meet me

70

if he had not made up his mind that you would suit."

"But *I* am not so sure!" The cry came from Dillon's constricted spirit.

"Of course not. It is too soon. There, I have rung for tea. Randolph would not want me to hector you, and I hope I haven't, but once you become a mother you will understand my feelings. Tell me, Mrs. Sample, how long did you live with your husband before his death?"

"Not quite a year, I think."

"Think? You cannot remember?"

Dillon could have wept with joy when the door opened to admit Herblock and his retinue of footmen. The tea table was got ready, light draperies were drawn across a portion of the octagonal, plant-filled solarium in which they sat, and the servants retired to take up a position just outside in the hall. Dillon accepted her cup and prayed that the rest of company might appear at once.

"Mrs. Sample, tell me about your husband." The dowager was sweetly unrelenting. "Did you love him very much?"

Dillon could bear the strain no longer.

"I am not Mrs. Matilda Sample," she confessed, putting aside her cup as if she had been poisoned. "I am Miss Dillon Hearn, sister to Caroline's father. I have never married. I am here in this disguise only because the real Matilda Sample fell ill at the last minute and Caroline refused to accept anyone else as her companion. I am ashamed that the conventions have forced me to assume the title of a married woman—as if at almost thirty I am too lacking in worldly wisdom to guard my niece from harm! However, I can only apologize to you for my deception and beg you not to reveal the truth to anyone."

The older woman sat in silence. With a searching look, she caught Dillon's eye and delved into her innermost recesses. Slowly a smile moved like sunlight across her worn features.

"I knew there was something amiss. Don't worry. I shall not tell a soul, except perhaps my son."

"Must you? I would rather leave matters as they stand."

"Not yet, at any rate. Let us see how things go on. Come now. Have some cake and stop looking like a hunted doe. You need not marry Randolph or any man if it does not suit you."

At that moment the door to the garden flung open, and Arabella Worthing entered flushed and laughing with her adoring suitor, lanky, serious Sir John, following at her heels. Behind them a moment later trailed Caroline, golden in pale yellow. She was not laughing. Instead she wore an expression of guarded consciousness as if the man at her side had made a meaningful remark to her which had left her either disturbed or thoughtful.

Roxbury again! Dillon's cup clattered in its saucer, but she made herself smile and appear amiable while the young couples seated themselves and took their plates. The sunlight slanting in made the most of Roxbury's scarred temple and the deep grooves beside his mouth, and it even caught out a trace of gray in his brown hair. He was not as young as he pretended. Caroline might almost have been his daughter.

Lost in thought as she was, it was only later that the import of their light conversation impinged on Dillon's mind. She sat up straighter.

"A picnic? I think it unwise," she pronounced with every sign of firmness. "It is certain to rain tomorrow."

Arabella clasped her hands together and turned to her entreatingly. It was plain that she and Sir John had come to some sort of understanding, and she had trouble containing her spirits.

"Oh, Mrs. Sample, it *cannot* rain tomorrow! It dare not! The duke has promised us a famous ride cross-country to view his Roman ruins. *Please* say it will not rain."

Before Dillon could speak the door to the terrace opened to admit the duke, accompanied by a lively pair of setters who promptly knocked a fern off its stand and sniffed among the shards, barking so ecstatically that the dowager had to raise her voice to make herself heard.

"Take Castor and Pollux outside again at once, Randolph! There, I warned you."

Lord and Lady Neville, ushered in from the hall by Herblock, were greeted by the larger of the two dogs with so much enthusiasm that the unsteady nobleman was bowled over onto his back, while the lady stood by wringing her thin hands and moaning.

Orders were delivered, bells rung, and burnt feathers fetched for Lady Isabel. Two footmen assisted Lord Neville into a chair, where he subsided panting and accepted a large glass of brandy with a piteous sigh of relief.

The Daunt family, arriving after the Nevilles, expressed their shock at the accident which, they declared, would never have been permitted to happen in India. The duke, having taken a seat beside Dillon, shouted to his servants for help.

"Get the dogs out of here, Herblock!"

The butler rushed to the rescue of a small table just too late. The china shepherdess crashed under the sweep of Pollux's plumy tail.

Dillon raised her handkerchief to her lips to hide her welling mirth.

"I fear that Mrs. Sample is overcome. Shall I call for more burnt feathers, madam?"

It was Roxbury's oily smooth voice coming from behind her, and indignation helped her to pull herself together. "I am quite well, Lord Roxbury." Her lips quivered with remembered fun, but she firmed them sternly. "It is Caroline who looks pale. Come, let us walk out to the terrace, dear child. Fresh air will ease you."

"I have already taken the air, Mrs. Sample. Now I am enjoying this delicious cake."

When Caroline turned stubborn there was no moving her, yet she had somehow to be prized from Roxbury's side long enough for Dillon to make it clear that the planned picnic would not suit. If Roxbury should get her alone in a romantic setting, anything might happen.

"It is delightfully cool on the terrace," she said, getting up and going toward the door.

Instead of Caroline, the duke bounced up and joined her.

"What's this nonsense about not going to the ruins?" he demanded in a testy tone. "I made the arrangements only to please you. You cannot disappoint me now."

"It would be too exhausting for Miss Daunt. She says she is not accustomed to riding."

"A jaunt of barely an hour is not likely to tire even the most feeble young lady, and Miss Daunt looks to be in perfect health. Ho—what's happening?"

For an uproar had broken out behind their backs. They watched as Herblock and Purk, one of the footmen, herded the two dogs toward the terrace door where they stood, though not without much barking on the one side and muttered threats on the other. The duke opened the door hastily, but just as they appeared ready to force the animals outside, Castor turned on Herblock and bared his teeth. Purk, having reached for Pollux's collar, withdrew his hand to stare at a long scratch on its back.

Masters of their fate again, the setters bounded across the room barking proudly. They discovered the tea table and descended upon it with whines of delight to lap up cakes and sandwiches indiscriminately.

Arabella and Caroline collapsed against each other, helpless with laughter. Miss Daunt emitted a steady low scream. Sir John ran across and grabbed at Castor's collar, only to stare after the animal ruefully as he soared out of reach over the tea table, scattering cups and cakes with his tail.

"Herblock, I told you to get those dogs out of here!" the duke thundered above the commotion.

"They do not wish to go, Your Grace," the bedeviled butler panted.

Dillon stood watching as the duke, joined by Sir John and Lord Roxbury, gave chase around the room. It was all wonderfully funny, but when she looked at the dowager and saw that she was genuinely upset, Dillon acted promptly. The piercing whistle she produced with two fingers, her tongue, and plenty of air brought Castor and Pollux galloping to her side eagerly.

The door was still open. In firm tones she commanded the dogs to come along with her. Once outside with them, she knelt and hugged each of them in turn and bade them to sit. Feathery tails thumping, they obeyed, whereupon she gave each one a comfortable tickle along the ribs that left them her fawning slaves.

The rest of the party had poured out onto the terrace and stood watching, excepting Lord Neville, who had fallen into a doze in his chair.

"Well done, Mrs. Sample," the dowager commended. "Purk, get leashes and remove those naughty creatures to the kennel. Herblock, we'll leave you to clear away the debris while we stroll down to the Italian garden. Randolph, I have made up my mind to accompany you to the ruins tomorrow after all. I haven't enjoyed a house party so much in years."

As Dillon rose to her feet and Purk fastened on the dogs' leashes, she heard Miss Daunt say to her mother in a sibilant whisper, "Surely it cannot be proper for a lady to whistle in that shocking fashion, can it, Mama?"

"I could scarcely believe my ears! But she is an American, and I have heard it said that the country is hardly civilized as yet."

Dillon turned away and found herself facing Lord Roxbury. A wry smile wreathed his lips.

"Miss Daunt," he said in his cold voice, "Mrs. Sample has refused to sanction the picnic tomorrow out of kindness toward you. She fears the ride will overtire you. I suggest that you go in the carriage with the dowager and your mama. Mortimer will want to ride, but we will all meet at the ruins."

"I will ride too. I only wish I had known of the plan so Papa could have sent my dependable Grayling ahead for me to ride."

"I believe my stables are capable of providing a suitable mount for you, Miss Daunt," the duke said, incensed.

"Of course, Your Grace!" Mrs. Daunt threw herself into the breach. "No one could doubt it after a single day's visit to your magnificent estate! Only in India have I seen anything as handsome . . ."

"You are too kind, Mrs. Daunt."

The dowager reached for the duke's arm. Together they led the procession of guests down shallow steps and across the luscious greensward toward the Italian garden. Looking around for Caroline, Dillon saw the girl walking between Arabella and Sir John, listening as they both talked to her at once. Before she could move to catch up, Roxbury took her arm and guided her across the lawn decorously.

"I suppose I must thank you for giving the Daunts a setdown, Lord Roxbury."

"It was nothing. By the by, if you truly do not wish to join the excursion tomorrow, you need not.

77

Since the dowager has agreed to come along, we are provided with a quorum of chaperones."

So that was his scheme, Dillon thought: first to disarm her and then, when he got Caroline to himself, to propose whatever it was he had in mind for the girl. Surely not a *carte blanche*? Not even Roxbury would dare to go so far. Or would he?

Dillon tilted back her head and stared Roxbury in the eye. Gray and blue met in steely confrontation.

"I go wherever Caroline goes. Depend upon it, my lord."

CHAPTER FIVE

The dowager and her older guests were to be driven to the ruins in comfortable style, while Herblock and his minions filled a second vehicle, and the hampers of food were to be transported in a wide farm cart.

Those who rode, having been severely catechized by the duke as to their various capabilities, gathered in the drive while grooms brought around the horses. Dillon, dressed in a new and modish dark blue habit trimmed daringly in green velvet, was helped into her saddle first.

"Sheba was Mama's favorite when she rode regularly," the duke declared as a groom led forward a beautiful tawny mare. "She's not used to strangers, but Mama thought you could handle her."

He gave Dillon a toss into the saddle. Sheba rolled her eyes and danced sideways nervously. Dillon leaned over and stroked her arched neck. "Softly, my pretty. Calm yourself until we get to know each other, and then we'll have a good run." Sheba snorted but gradually grew quiet.

The duke, appearing relieved, went off to attend to the others. Caroline and Arabella mounted capably, but Miss Daunt, lifted into the saddle by a perspiring Mortimer and a groom, hauled so hard on the reins that the sedate animal she had been allotted reared slightly in surprise at being so mistreated. It took two grooms to calm the beast and Mortimer's best efforts to persuade Miss Daunt that all would be well if she let her mount have his head.

Caroline and Roxbury fell in behind Dillon and the duke. Arabella and Sir John followed, and last came Mortimer, shepherding the anxious Miss Daunt, his complexion somewhat redder than usual. The duke led them at a modest pace through tree-bordered glades, across rolling fields and pastureland, skirting a wooded belt that undulated with the contours of the land like a dark green ribbon on a bodice.

"Yes, it's good land," the duke agreed when Dillon praised its beauty. "Queer thing, that both of my wives loathed coming to Benwell. They were city-bred, pretty as doves, both of them, and they preferred cards and balls to mussing their coiffures out of doors." A horn sounded ahead. "That will be Ferris with the carts. I'd best ride on ahead to make sure all is in train. Roxbury, will you and Miss Hearn accompany Mrs. Sample the rest of the way?"

Caroline threw her aunt a naughty side glance as she and Roxbury cantered up to join Dillon. "Benwell is an impressive estate. Invite me often in the future," she whispered just as Roxbury caught with them up. She turned to him with a melting smile. "If your Botham Abbey is half as

80

lovely, I wonder how you gentlemen can bear to leave ever."

"Botham Abbey is nearly as handsome, or so I think, but, like Benwell, it lacks a feminine presence. The duke and I go to London, Miss Hearn, when we grow starved for a glimpse of another kind of beauty."

Caroline, who had heard the duke lamenting his wives' devotion to the city, caught him up. "But when you marry, you discover that your wives loathe the country. I wonder why people do not discuss their preferences before marriage."

Dillon had been pondering the matter too. "There must be a reason why some women cannot be happy in such idyllic surroundings."

"I fear there are several," Roxbury replied blandly. Dillon caught the gleam of mischief in his blue eyes and berated herself for having given him an opening. "In England we expect a great deal of our wives. They must entertain large parties at a moment's notice, ride well, have a care for the servants and our tenants, and, of course, give birth to a suitable number of offspring, preferably males. Aside from these requirements, we do naturally expect them to appear handsome at all times, never to fall into fits of depression or moods or tempers, and to gratify us in all our requirements."

Dillon's indignation flared out of control at his last words.

"No wonder they die off in such a hurry!"

"Lord Roxbury was roasting you, Mrs. Sample," Caroline interposed, reining in beside Sheba. "Don't be unkind. Remember that Lord Roxbury has lost his wife, and the duke has lost two."

81

"Under the circumstances, that is not surprising!" Dillon retorted.

Caroline said a silent prayer of gratitude upon seeing the duke riding toward them at that moment.

"What's this? You're all in a taking, Mrs. Sample. Has someone offended you?" He turned a ferocious frown on Roxbury.

"Certainly not." Dillon choked back her fury with an effort. "I am only over-warm. Let us ride on ahead."

She touched Sheba with her knees, and her anger dissipated as the mare began to gallop. Her hat flew off and her hair streamed around her head, but she was laughing again by the time she drew up beside the duke at the banks of a narrow stream. Across on the other side the duke pointed out a flat-topped hill which commanded a view over a green meadow sprinkled prodigally with wildflowers.

"Part of the old Roman road ran through this meadow. The fort sat atop that hill. My tenants sometimes turn up bits of metal or pottery in the fields round about."

"There is not much left standing."

"The walls have been vandalized for generations. You can see Roman bricks in the old tower at Benwell."

"How quickly time erases the past," Dillon sighed.

"So we must enjoy life while we can." The duke's eyes kindled, and he reached for her hand. "Mrs. Sample, you are too young to waste—"

"Oh, here are Miss Hearn and Lord Roxbury approaching," Dillon cried. Freeing her hand, she pitched her voice in parlor accents. "Yes, only imagine how different the history of England would have been if Rome had not fallen to the Vandals."

The duke frowned. "What, and let a lot of Italians govern our country? We would never stand for it, never!"

Torn between laughter and a sharp retort, Dillon instead followed the duke meekly across a ford in the stream and up the gentle bank into the flowery meadow, where they found the dowager and her other guests had arrived before them. The dowager sat in a chair her maid had placed in the shade of an ancient oak at the edge of the meadow and watched benignly as the young people dismounted and walked about gathering daisies and exclaiming over the blue of the cornflowers.

Arabella and Sir John wandered after the others, holding hands like children in an enchanted land, while Mortimer trailed in Miss Daunt's wake carrying a straggling bouquet of dying blooms she had thrust upon him. Dillon kept Caroline at her side in spite of the duke's hopeful suggestions that they were sure to find prettier flowers in the wood or down by the stream. Roxbury strolled along on Caroline's other side. Dillon could not help noticing that he was highly entertained by the duke's efforts to get her to himself.

A summons from the dowager soon recalled them to partake of the feast Herblock and his minions had arranged upon temporary tables. There were pink hams, tureens of vegetables fresh from the gardens, roasted fowl, sirloins of beef, and heaping trays of fruits and pastries. Footmen spread robes or placed chairs for those unable to sit upon the ground. Indeed, Caroline whispered to Dillon over a lobster patty, poor Lord Neville was hardly able to remain upright in a chair.

The hearty buffet finished, guests replete, the ladies raised parasols, and Mr. Daunt fell into a doze, the flesh bulging above his tight collar. The duke, too, appeared to be ready for a nap, Dillon thought hopefully. Instead he pulled himself up smartly and announced that it was time to view the ruins.

"Come along, Mrs. Sample!" he ordered.

"I long to see the ruins too," Arabella declared.

"I too," Caroline said.

"Well, you may join us if you do not mind the climb," the duke told them ungraciously.

So it was that, led by the duke with Dillon at his side, the three young couples started up the hill. When they reached the top, Miss Daunt and Mortimer were panting uncomfortably. The duke located a comfortable rock and sat down upon it, waving his hand toward the tumbled heap of broken masonry and shattered quarry stones that lay half concealed under weeds and lichen.

"You can see the outlines of the fort if you look close. Some say other forts were built atop the Roman one in later years. Fellows have dug into the hillside, and they report having found bones and armor and a coin or two."

Miss Daunt viewed the rubble with disappointment. "Why, it is nothing like so handsome or large as the ancient palaces in India."

Affronted, the duke declared that heathen ruins held no interest for him and that it was known to the world that Indian princes took many wives, which would explain why they required very large palaces in which to house them.

"Do I detect a note of envy in the duke's voice?" Dillon heard Roxbury whisper and saw Caroline's mouth shape itself into an irresistible smile.

"In India a prince's widows must burn themselves on his funeral pyre," Miss Daunt advised them solemnly. "I witnessed one such suttee. It was so dreadful I was ill for a day afterward."

"Your sensibility does you credit," Roxbury told her, his tone suave and silky. "Burnley, may we walk around the place?"

"Only watch out for the sunken area inside the walls, and you are free to inspect all there is to see. The ground's loose in there where old foundations have weathered apart. Better stay on the outside where it's safe. Mrs. Sample, you sit here beside me, and I'll tell you a little of Benwell's history."

"You are kind, but since I have never seen anything so ancient as your Roman ruins I think I will accompany Miss Hearn and Lord Roxbury."

The duke struggled to his feet with a sigh. Together the four couples strolled around the perimeters of the old fort. Its crumbling walls were barely visible under mounds of earth and grass, though the outline of a large enclosed place still remained. They were halfway around when Miss Daunt interrupted the duke's historical monologue with a cry as sharp as a peacock's.

"I see something shiny there in the grass. It could be a Roman coin!"

"Hold on. Don't go over the wall. It's dangerous!" the duke bellowed in dismay.

But he was too late. Miss Daunt was already inside the enclosure and running with more haste than grace toward a rocky area half overgrown with weeds and wild grass.

"Come back at once, Henrietta!" Mortimer bawled.

Upon hearing his voice, Miss Daunt turned and hesitated, but her momentum carried her another step forward. Even as they watched, she was seen to step into a depression of some sort and fall forward with a cry of pain into the long grass.

"Stay back, all of you!" Roxbury ordered sharply. He leaped the wall and approached the prone girl, who had apparently fainted. Tersely he said, after having examined the circumstances, "Her foot is caught between a pair of stones. The whole area is loose and out of balance and may crush the foot if any weight is put on the surrounding stones. I believe I can free her, but I will need help. Mrs. Sample, you are the smallest. Take care as you approach."

With Roxbury giving out orders, Dillon negotiated the final few feet on her hands and knees, testing each inch of ground before putting her weight to it. It seemed an eternity before she knelt beside the victim and was able to assess the extent of the crisis. Miss Daunt's leg, encased in its leather riding boot, was trapped almost to her knee between two rough blocks of stone. Except for Roxbury's strained arms, which held back the larger stone, the foot would have been crushed gradually and inexorably.

Roxbury was sweating, his stock in total disarray, his lips closed in a grim line. She noticed that his hands were bleeding and his nostrils flared as he bent all his strength toward preventing the stones from closing.

"Reach in and take off her boot," he ordered Dillon in a suffocating voice.

Dillon, lying flat on her stomach, managed to slide one hand down inside the narrow opening, confident that Roxbury would not let the trap close on her or Miss Daunt. It was immediately apparent that the boot could not be removed.

"But if you can manage to pull that stone aside a fraction further," she muttered after a moment, "I think I can release her, boot and all. Ah, almost! Please try again, if you can," she pleaded as she felt the booted foot come half free.

He obeyed. Now there was room for Dillon to fasten her hand around the girl's ankle. At her side she could hear Roxbury taking painfully deep breaths as he made yet another effort to move the heavy block of stone. Dillon pulled, but the foot remained obstinately wedged. Probing into loose soil with her fingers, she turned the toe of the boot from side to side until she felt it come free from some encumbrance. "Quickly! Pull now!" she cried.

With a suddenness that caught Dillon entirely by surprise, Miss Daunt's foot came free. The girl's heavy body fell forward, and the heel of her boot shot up like a cannonball into Dillon's middle. She sat down so hard that she was unable to repress an unladylike grunt as the air went out of her momentarily.

An expression of unholy glee came over Roxbury's sweating countenance, but he only said, "I hope you are not hurt. Miss Daunt is coming around. You had better go back first, but be careful how you cross the stones. You'd not want to have the breath knocked out of you twice."

He waited until Dillon was safe on the wall, then picked up the moaning Miss Daunt and carried her back to safety. The duke cut away her boot and pronounced that her ankle was badly bruised but not broken. A pair of footmen appeared with a chair in which they carried the sobbing girl down the hill to the waiting coach, with Mortimer slipping and sliding anxiously in their wake, though not before he had drawn Roxbury aside to say bitterly, "You should have let me rescue Miss Daunt, Lord Roxbury, for we are soon to announce our engagement."

"Another time, Neville. My congratulations. If I were you, I would ride beside the carriage on the way back so that she will have the comfort of your presence."

Fists clenched, Mortimer slowly turned and started back down the hill. Roxbury swung around to the rest of the party with a smile.

"Now that Miss Daunt is in good hands, I suggest that we finish our inspection of the ruins. We who are riding can reach Benwell in half the time it will take the carriages. Perhaps one of us will even discover the coin Miss Daunt saw when she fell."

Dillon, unaware that her hair was blown hither and yon and that she had a smudge of dirt across one cheek, said calmly, "I have found it, and left it where it was. It was a bit of bone."

Arabella shivered. "How dreadful."

"I do not think so, Miss Worthing," Dillon said. "We are all part of this earth and must return to it one day. That Roman soldier is safely ensconced in a better world by this time."

Caroline caught a glint of mirth in Roxbury's observant eyes. Aunt Dill, assuming her authoritative schoolmistress tone, now went on to take command, quoting various historical sources, from Pliny to Shakespeare, as she prowled in and out of the ruins. As for the duke, he wore an expression of stunned admiration on his ruddy countenance as he followed at Dillon's heels.

"You're a bit of a bluestocking, Mrs. Sample," he said after she gave them a brief account of the Roman invasion of Britain. "Never had a notion they made your kind good to look at, though Mama was a beauty in her day and she was strong in the loft. Papa was used to say that he would rather look at her than listen to her."

"Like father, like son," Roxbury murmured *sotto voce* to Caroline as they began to descend the hill. "I never would have guessed that old Burnley could look so doting."

Caroline made a face. "I think him much too old for my dear Mrs. Sample. But love is seldom rational, is it?"

He looked down into her eyes meaningfully. "You are very young to be so wise. Have you learned from experience or from observation?"

"From both. I belong to a very happy family, Lord Roxbury. My parents—"

"Ah, here is the groom with your mount."

He handed Caroline into the saddle and went to mount himself, his face dark and closed.

CHAPTER SIX

Dinner that evening was subdued, the duke having been called to the bedside of his elderly agent who had suffered a stroke and was dying. The dowager sent word that she was weary after their excursion and would rest, while Miss Daunt was to have a tray in her room with her anxious mama in attendance. Lord Neville was announced to suffer from a vague indisposition that kept him prostrated.

Throughout the lengthy dinner Lady Neville and Mr. Daunt commiserated with each other over Miss Daunt's accident and excused themselves soon after the fruit was served to attend upon the injured girl. Sir John departed for London on a mysterious errand. Only Arabella, Caroline, and Dillon remained to drink tea in the drawing room. They had hardly settled with their cups when Arabella confided that Sir John had asked Lord Roxbury for permission to address her.

"He refused at first. Instead he sent for me and asked me my feelings. When I told him that I would have my John or no one for a husband, he agreed to talk Mama around. Best of all, he has settled

Morrowfield on us so that we shall be quite comfortable, even though we shall have to spend most of our time in the country. John has gone off to speak to his parents, and now I must go and write a note to Mama. She will agree to anything Uncle Charles decides. Oh, I am so awfully happy!" She ran away to her room.

Finding himself alone with Lord Roxbury after the ladies left, Mortimer, glancing uneasily at his saturnine companion, poured himself a generous glass of brandy and leaned his weak chin on his hand.

"Must apologize if I overspoke myself when Miss Daunt was hurt," he mumbled. "Worried, you know, and all that."

"Quite understandable. Let me congratulate you again on your betrothal. I hope your parents are pleased."

"Happy as grigs. They thought of Miss Hearn for me until Mama was put off by her behavior." Mortimer swallowed half his ration of brandy and coughed. "Though if Cousin Caro had shown me a little warmth I'd have offered for her in spite of Mama."

"You're a brave young man." If there was a sardonic gleam in Roxbury's blue eyes, Mortimer failed to notice. "Let me refill your glass. Excellent. Now tell me. What do you know about your cousin from America? If she is in truth your cousin, which some doubt."

Mortimer drank deeply before replying. "Oh, she's a cousin, all right. Mama looked her up in the family book. She's the granddaughter of a younger brother who went to the Colonies to repair his fortune. Did poorly, I understand, that is until his daughter married an excessively wealthy man. No title there, naturally, whereas I do not doubt that Mr. Daunt will be knighted for his services to the Crown. It won't be a hereditary title, like ours, but it is better than nothing."

"Just so. I wish you every happiness, though I have a notion that your future parents-in-law may not be easy to live with."

Mortimer sagged on his elbows. "Overpowerin' woman, Mrs. Daunt. The old man seems kind. Offered to set us up in our own town house and furnish it suitable to our consequence. They will live with us until we fill the nursery," he added gloomily.

"Brace up, Neville. I suggest twins to begin. More brandy? To get back to Miss Hearn, is it true that her father is engaged in trade? There have been rumors to that effect."

"Think she's not up to your touch, eh? Mama thinks there may be something havey-cavey about the Hearn fortune. Not that it ain't there, if that's what you want to know! Thing is, her papa is said to build the best vessels in the world in his ship-yards. Not quite a gentleman's occupation, but if you fancy Miss Hearn, you may count on me to keep mum. Fifty thousand and one of the most beautiful ... If only m'mama had seen different ..."

Mortimer's head sank down slowly upon his arms, and a long snore emanated from him. Lord Roxbury rang for Herblock, quitting the room in relief as soon as the butler entered.

In the meantime, after Arabella left them, Caroline and Dillon sat together somewhat tentatively in the large, formal drawing room, which was hardly warmed of the evening chill by a distant blaze in a massive fireplace.

"I wonder whether I would like to make my home in England, Aunt Dill." Caroline put her cup in its saucer and sighed pensively. "If it is this cold in May, imagine what winter must be."

Ignoring the gooseflesh along her own arms, Dillon said briskly, "I believe the climate is moderate the year round, although one does notice the damp in these lovely old buildings. However, we need not consider the matter since we will be returning home in September."

"Will we? Are you sure you won't have the duke when he offers?"

"I shall do my possible to discourage him. If he persists, of course I shall refuse. I am more concerned over what *you* will do when Lord Roxbury offers. I cannot believe that you will be happy with such a man, Caroline."

"I am not sure either. Do admit, though, that he is above everyone the most interesting man we have met in England as well as the most handsome."

"Are you so deep in love with Roxbury that you are blind to his faults? He is a cold, cynical man, interested in nothing beyond his own pleasures. I wish I could be sure that he is not trifling with your affections. I beg you not to succumb to his practiced blandishments, child."

Caroline sighed again. On this night her beauty seemed oddly dimmed. She stared into the fire and made no answer.

Dillon's first impulse was to comfort her. If Caroline was truly in love, perhaps it was wrong to interfere. Roxbury might have changed, have grown more dependable and kind. It would be nothing strange if he had fallen deep in love with Caroline, for her lovely surface was a reflection of her calm, sweet inner nature.

At this moment, Herblock ushered in Lord Roxbury himself. At sight of his confident smile, all the sympathy Dillon had begun to feel drained away in a rush.

"I regret to advise you that Mortimer is unwell and will not join the ladies this evening." He strolled across the room toward Dillon, who sat behind the tea table. "May I have a cup in spite of being shamefully late? Miss Hearn, I have never had the pleasure of hearing you play or sing. Will you go to the piano and do your best to lift my spirits after my tête-à-tête with young Mortimer?"

"With pleasure," said Caroline readily, her smile sunny again. While she looked over the music, Roxbury sat on the hard sofa at Dillon's side and leaned back in an attitude of total relaxation.

Caroline selected a piece and launched into a sprightly Scottish ballad. Hands folded in the lap of her gray velvet gown trimmed demurely in black, Dillon gave every indication of listening with rapt attention.

"Fraud," Roxbury challenged. "You are longing to tell me exactly what you think of me and I know it."

"Caroline plays excellently, does she not?"

"Caroline—let us talk of her. You are doing your possible to put obstacles in my way. This is my first chance to ask you why."

"To begin, you are far too old and experienced for her!"

"She may be young in years but not in understanding. She was born wise, whereas it took me thirty-five years to acquire a modicum of wisdom. Therefore we have arrived at the same goal together despite the difference in our ages."

"There is more than your age against you. To put it bluntly, your reputation is not of the highest."

An unholy grin touched his lips and was gone.

"If it pleases you to call me a rake, you have my permission to do so. I can assure you that if I marry, I expect to be the perfect model of a husband."

Dillon pounced. "*If* you marry! That is precisely the point. How am I to believe that you are not just trifling—?"

Caroline's song came to a sudden end, and she sat waiting for their approval.

"That was lovely, dear child," Dillon said out of the silence. "Come back and sit with us now."

Roxbury protested. "Only a single song? Your voice is rarely soft and soothing, Miss Hearn. Please do not stop yet."

"As you wish." Caroline ran her fingers over the keys and launched into a pretty French song which suited the small range of her voice.

"Your niece," Roxbury said lazily, "is the most enchanting young lady I have come across in a dozen years. I find it difficult to believe that she is an offshoot of the same Hearn family I came to know as a very young man. Perhaps her mother's influence saved her from . . . ?"

Dillon whispered fiercely, "She has never known

unhappiness. If you dare to hurt her, I promise I shall find a way to make you suffer for it!"

He raised his eyebrows. "I should not like to meet you in a duel, Mrs. Sample. Gentlemen rarely shoot to kill, you know. It is not in our code."

"Women live by a different code. Since we are forbidden to use weapons, we learn to practice guile instead."

"Then I am safe. You could not hoodwink the merest schoolboy, I believe. You have not got the face for guilt."

Dillon bent suddenly to fiddle with the teapot in order to hide an angry blush.

"I had forgotten how you flush up when you're in a temper," Roxbury remarked, crossing his elegantly clad legs and swinging his perfectly shod foot with an air of pleasure. "Now you are even hotter. You haven't learned to deal with it after all these years. Didn't Mr. Sample ever tease you?"

"Of course not. *He* was a gentleman."

"Tell me more about your dear departed spouse. Was he very brilliant as well as being plump in the pocket? I am sure he must have been a man of easy temperament, since he chose to marry you."

"He was a man who kept his promises, which is more than I can say for you!"

Caroline's song trailed off softly. Roxbury, clapping his hands together, sat up and requested an encore. Caroline appeared ready to agree until Dillon rose and said in a repressive voice, "It grows late. Caroline, come along. We have promised to be up early in the morning to help the dowager prepare for the ball tomorrow."

Roxbury bowed them out of the room. He bent

over Caroline's hand lingeringly while Dillon stalked through the door without a word or a backward glance.

"Did Lord Roxbury say something to offend you, Aunt Dilly?" Caroline asked as they climbed the staircase toward their rooms.

"Yes. No, I suppose not. It is just that there is something about that man that irritates me beyond measure. He did not ask for your hand, if that is what you are wondering."

They had arrived at the upper hall, where their adjoining rooms were situated. Caroline halted with her hand on the latch of her door.

"I believe that Lord Roxbury would apply to my cousin, Lord Neville, rather than to you, if he means to make me an offer. Should Lord Neville give his consent, it will be my decision to accept him or not."

Too surprised to speak, Dillon stared at the girl. Caroline said good night with a cool little smile and, going through the door, shut it firmly behind her.

Dillon went along to her own room forlornly and sank down on the floor before the fire. What had she done? In her effort to save Caroline from being hurt, she had estranged her beloved niece.

After some uneasy struggles with her conscience, she made up her mind that she must tell Caroline the truth about Roxbury and her own relationship with him, admit that she had been quickly won and as quickly discarded by the same Charles Norton who was now known as Lord Roxbury. But not yet! One had one's pride. She would do it later, if matters came to the point.

It was long before she fell asleep that night despite the hot milk Emerald brought her. The goose-down pillows kept slipping from her grasp, and her dreams were equally unsettled. When she awakened early the next morning, she got out of bed with a sense of relief and crept downstairs to walk in the shrubbery until she felt herself again.

Arriving in the dining room for breakfast, she found Caroline already there and the duke half finished but full of solicitude.

"You don't look at all the thing, Mrs. Sample. Can't have you puny, not here at Benwell, where the air is as pure as our spring waters. Come along and let me help you fill your plate."

He helped her from a gargantuan array of dishes both hot and cold upon the sideboard, ignoring her protests that she was not very hungry. A footman carried her heaped plate back to the long dining table.

"I must say that I like to see a lady display a hearty appetite," Lord Roxbury remarked, strolling into the dining room just as Dillon sat down before her plate. He was clad in the most exquisite cut coat and breeches Dillon had ever seen, although it must be admitted that the wide shoulders and fine figure displayed owed nothing to his tailors. Caroline could hardly be blamed for admiring the outer man. It was the inner one who was despicable.

Mr. Daunt came pounding into the room with his buxom wife on Roxbury's heels. "I agree with you, Lord Roxbury. Can't abide meeching females myself. Shall I help you, my love, or do you prefer . . . ?"

Mrs. Daunt had already made for the buffet. She

filled her plate with little coos of pleasure, though when she and her husband began to eat, their voracity struck the others into silence. It was Caroline, pretty-mannered as always, who broke the spell.

"I trust our expedition yesterday was not too much for your mama," she said, addressing the duke. "She is remarkable. To run this vast estate must be a heavy responsibility."

"I don't know how I would go on without her, Miss Hearn. Poor Wilkins died last night, you know, and he and Mama between them managed everything. I told Mama to look about at once for a suitable replacement. She has already sent to talk to a man she heard recommended highly. I am to interview him on Tuesday."

"Too bad, Burnley. That means you will not be coming to Botham Abbey with us," Roxbury commented.

The duke's ruddy face was disconcerted.

"So it does, confound it! However, we will enjoy ourselves while we may. Mrs. Sample, you promised to ride into the village with me this morning to examine the tombs in the old church."

"I'm sorry, but I cannot. I'm needed to help your mama with the flowers for the ballroom."

"The flowers can wait until afternoon," the duke complained. "They'll keep fresher that way."

"But Miss Hearn has said she does not wish to ride, and I cannot leave her alone." Dillon threw an agonized glance across the table toward her niece which Caroline avoided.

"I have guaranteed to keep Miss Daunt company

this morning so I shall be safely occupied, dear Mrs. Sample."

Roxbury stood up. "Capital idea to visit the tombs, duke. I've no plans at all for the morning and will be happy to join you and Mrs. Sample. What time do we start?"

The riding party returned late for the nuncheon that they found the rest of the guests enjoying alfresco on the broad terrace of Benwell. The tiny dowager presided, while her maid held a parasol over her head to shelter her from the unexpectedly warm sun. Only Miss Daunt was missing. Her mother explained in reply to Dillon's civil inquiry that she had ordered the girl to stay abed until evening so that she would be in her best looks when she was carried down to lie on a chaise in the ballroom to watch the gaiety.

Dillon excused herself to go to her room and freshen up, noting as she washed that the tilted tip of her nose had got slightly burned by the sun. Ah well. It was not as if she were a beauty, after all.

When she returned to the terrace, she found Caroline talking to a handsome young man not far from her in age who seemed unable to take his eyes off her. Dillon cheered silently. More competition for Roxbury!

The duke arrived from his own suite shortly after Dillon. At sight of the new arrival, he came to a sudden halt.

"What are *you* doing here?" The doting smile he had assumed for Dillon changing to a ferocious glare. "That's my son, Winfield," he explained to Dillon aside, "supposed to be up at Oxford when last I heard. Don't tell me you've been sent down again?"

The young man wrenched his gaze from Caroline with reluctance.

"Not this time, sir. I—er—I was anxious to see you and my grandmama."

The duke cleared his throat angrily. "How much this time? If you imagine you can continue to live like a demmed rajah at my expense, then let me tell you that . . ."

"Randolph!" The dowager's voice cut off her son's diatribe suddenly. "It is fortunate that Winfield arrived in time for our ball tonight," she went on, smiling across at her grandson. "There are always too many girls. Winfield will do his duty and partner every one in turn."

They all laughed at his woeful countenance. "Not Charlotte and Letty both, Grandmama?"

"Both! We have invited all our neighbors except those who are still in town, so you will be kept busy. Of course you must partner our house guests as well."

"Willingly!" Winfield drew a chair close to Caroline's and could be heard asking how many dances she would give him.

"Yours are all taken," Caroline teased.

"Never believe it. Two of my friends are on their way to Benwell, and I'll put them to work tonight. Pym may have Letty, and I'll give Charlotte to Stafford. I am known throughout Oxford for my generosity, Miss Hearn."

They could not help laughing at the brash young man, even the duke, whose amusement was tempered by a frown of responsibility.

"I won't have that rackety Pym cutting a swath among our country girls, or you either," he warned.

"Hear, hear!" Roxbury was laughing. "I never guessed you were such a tyrant in the bosom of your family, Burnley."

The duke's son grinned engagingly. "Oh, we don't mind father, sir. It's only to worry when Grandmama flies up into the boughs."

"Which is what I shall do unless you give up your chair to Lord Roxbury and find another for yourself at once," the dowager said. "Mrs. Sample, come here and sit by me. I've been sent a book by a Miss Jane Austen. Have you heard of it?"

"If you refer to *Pride and Prejudice*, indeed I have! It is a delightful comedy of manners which you are bound to enjoy."

Arabella said it had made her laugh so heartily that she had got the hiccups, at which statement Sir John, back from London, looked faint with solicitude. The Daunts declaring that they did not approve of reading novels, the conversation languished before it turned to preparations for the ball.

The afternoon had dwindled by half by the time the dowager took Dillon and Caroline away to the greenhouses with her. There they chose great masses of flowers to decorate the ballroom, which, Dillon decided when a footman opened its doors for her, must be of a size to contain two tennis courts at once. An undergardener who had been sent out to cut branches of fragrant lilac and tall, shiny stalks of rhododendron leaves, which Dillon and Caroline arranged in large urns at the four corners of the room. Palms were banked around the musicians' platform. Hothouse lilies and tuberoses drenched in perfume were placed in smaller containers on tables set among the dainty chairs that lined the frescoed walls.

"I have never seen this barn of a room appear so handsome," the dowager praised. "Randolph's wives always left the flowers to the servants. While my husband lived, I loved arranging them myself, but now that he is gone I seldom take the trouble. Now you must go and rest so that you will look your best this evening."

They had hardly closed the door in Dillon's room when she turned on Caroline hotly. "Traitor! How could you have let me go off alone between the duke and Roxbury!"

"I believed that Roxbury would serve as the perfect chaperone. Don't tell me that the duke managed to declare himself in spite of Roxbury?"

"Of course not. Roxbury never left us alone for a moment. I must admit that I am grateful to him, for the duke is not easily put off, especially in the gloom of a crypt." Dillon sank down on the hearth rug with a little shiver. "Though it was indeed fascinating to examine the sculpted faces of earlier Burnleys atop the marble sarcophagi. One who died at the age of twenty-two was the image of young Winfield. Do you like him, Caro?"

"Oh, I find him great fun." Caroline sank down beside Dillon and hugged her knees pensively. "Win wants me to have supper with him, but I believe Lord Roxbury expects me to be his partner. I shall have to make a choice."

Caroline was still undecided when they descended the stairs that evening to stand with the duke and the dowager, the Nevilles, and the Daunts to greet the invited guests. Dillon responded quickly to the open faces and relaxed manners of these country people, who struck her as being very different from the members of the *ton* she had met in London, and they embraced her from the beginning almost as one of their own.

The last guests were passing through the receiving line when Sir Peter Porter, deaf in both ears, inquired in a voice audible throughout the room, "Is it this Mrs. Sample whom Randolph has got in mind for his third wife, Duchess? She's a touch on the slim side to foal easily, but he has got two heirs already so he can afford to enjoy this one, eh?"

From the corner of her eye, Dillon could see Roxbury savoring her discomfiture. "I could murder him!" she muttered between her teeth to Caroline.

"The poor man can't help being deaf."

"Not Sir Peter. Roxbury."

The duke helped his mother to her seat. "You may begin," he directed the musicians imperiously, after he had taken Dillon's arm and led her out onto the floor. Roxbury followed with Caroline on his arm, then Sir John with Arabella, and Winfield with Letty, a look of decorous suffering on his countenance.

It was a country dance. Having accustomed herself to the langorous posturing at London balls, Caroline was slow to enter into the gaiety, but it was not long before the vigor and relaxed enjoyment among the dancers infected her and she bounced and whirled and stomped with the best of them. Her golden skin aglow, she chided Roxbury when they went down the line together.

"You wear an air of aloofness, sir, as if you consider yourself above the company."

"Perhaps I am."

"How sad, for you. Fortunately, *I* am not. I rejoice to see people behave in a natural, carefree fashion, uninhibited by a fear of being out of the mode. Are you a Cynic, Lord Roxbury?"

"Either that or I am too old to enjoy frolicking in the same witless way I did at twenty." The music ended and he led her off the floor. "I hope you will have supper with me, Miss Hearn."

"I think—no, I think I will *not*, Lord Roxbury. I am unwilling to have my happy mood damped. There are a dozen ladies saying their prayers to have you as a partner so I need not worry that you will be left to pine alone."

"You are thoughtful for my comfort. Which lady shall I honor with an invitation?"

"I wish you would ask Mrs. Sample, for you and she are of an age and have much in common, but the duke is sure to have bespoken the supper dance. Still, you might put it to the touch."

"What, and risk another of her setdowns? Even I am not up to such a fate despite what Mrs. Sample calls my inflated self-esteem. No, you must leave it to me to find my own partner."

Meanwhile Dillon struggled through a duty dance with heavy-footed Mr. Daunt. Later she sat out a set to visit with Miss Daunt, who lay on a chaise with her injured limb propped on a low pillow, while Mortimer followed the dowager's instructions to dance with Charlotte.

However, Dillon did not lack for partners later. Having listened to the dowager attentively and compared her information with experience gathered at Hearn Hill, she was able to discuss crops, tenants' problems, and drains as comfortably as if she had lived in the country all her life.

"You're as light as a wisp," Sir Oswald Parvis commended Dillon, leading her back to her chair after a lively galop. "I must speak to my steward about your suggestions."

Dillon had scarce time to sit down and draw a breath before Sir Peter Porter's voice boomed out across the hall.

"Randolph has picked a winner this time! Excuse me. Must go and wangle a dance with her if I can."

It was a waltz which Dillon had already, in duty bound, promised to Lord Roxbury. That gentleman approached her rather hurriedly and bowed, but Sir Peter was before him.

"Age before beauty, Roxbury—not that you're a beauty with that scar on your phiz, eh, Mrs. Sample? Take my arm, dear lady. Don't hang back like a green girl. No need to look back over your shoulder. Roxbury don't mind."

And off Sir Peter took her to circle the floor like a pair of moths made mad by the myriad of candle flames until Dillon's normally steady head began to spin.

"May we slow down a bit, if you please?" she shouted into the ear she prayed was his better one.

"You want a bit of a squeeze, you say?" His long, houndlike face beamed. "You've chosen the right partner, dear lady. Ready? Here we go 'round again. What a small waist you have, Mrs. Sample."

Dillon began to believe that the music would never come to an end. When Sir Peter released her at last, she murmured that she might repair a flounce and, rid of him at last, staggered out through an open door that led to a balcony. There she found a seat on a stone balustrade and sat fanning herself, at first sick with humiliation until she imagined what a picture she and Sir Peter must have made, and then she could not stop chuckling.

Inside, the musicians struck up. She was to have danced with Mortimer, but she felt no compunction about absenting herself until she could regain her composure and cool her hot face.

Looking out across the lawn and garden, she saw a thin crescent moon admiring its image in the ornamental lake. Curving beds rich with fragrant bloom stood out against clipped borders of dark yew. On three sides, in the distance, a shadowy forest of oak and beech as old as parts of the Castle bounded the Benwell home grounds.

It was all very beautiful. To become mistress of this handsome estate would restore the sense of fulfillment which had been sadly lacking in her life since her father had died and the Latin School fallen into the hands of strangers. However, for the duke she could feel no more than friendship. Perhaps the kind of love she had experienced as a girl only happened among the young and naive. Most marriages appeared to her to be based on compromise.

"Mentally rearranging the gardens, Mrs. Sample?" It was Roxbury, and she wondered how long he had stood watching her. She slid down and faced him defensively, annoyed that he seemed to tower above her. "Forgive me if I disturbed you, Mrs.

Sample. You were gone so long that I feared you were overcome by your galop with Sir Peter."

"You need not concern yourself about me. The duke . . ."

"Happens to be dancing with Lady Neville. If it eases you, I can report that they both appeared morose."

"Credit him with doing his duty, at least."

"I do, I assure you. Whenever I am in residence at Botham Abbey, I dance with all my prettier guests. The homely ones I fob off onto poor old Forster."

"As you did when you sent him to dance with me at your ball, I suppose."

"That was not my doing. Miss Hearn conceived the notion that you would suit because you have books in common."

"Your concern for me is misplaced, as you have noticed. Should I ever wish to marry, I will choose my own candidate. I can take care of myself."

"So I have learned. May I escort you back to the ballroom? Supper is about to be served and you will be missed."

She hesitated a second before putting her hand on his arm. It was nothing but anger that made her tremble, she told herself fiercely. Certainly not that other childish emotion she had almost forgotten.

"Are you cold?" Lord Roxbury inquired solicitously.

"Perhaps a little." She would die rather than let him believe that she had any regard left for him. "Here is the duke coming toward us. You are free to devote yourself to more interesting pursuits now."

He bowed and turned away abruptly. In anger? She hoped so. To hurt him assuaged her old, unforgotten pain by an iota.

The duke complained that he was hot and tired. Obviously he was irked as well. "Never saw a woman so hard to catch and corner as you are, Mrs. Sample," he complained as he led her toward the supper room. "What were you doing out there with Roxbury?"

"I was not out there *with* him. I went outside for a breath of air after my strenuous dance with Sir Peter, and Roxbury came after me to make sure I was all right, no doubt because Caroline asked him to."

"I don't like the way he looks at you," the duke declared peevishly.

"It is my belief that he is working up his courage to ask my permission to address Caroline."

"I fear you're far out, Mrs. Sample. Roxbury don't lack courage, whatever else is amiss with the fellow. I wish I had as much." The duke's eyes kindled and he pressed her hand hotly. "Later . . ."

"Yes, later. I'm famished." They had entered the supper room. The dowager spied them and beckoned Dillon to come and sit at her side. "Do fill my plate with whatever you think I will like best while I talk with your mama."

Following her orders, the duke frowned over the choice between a lobster patty and a venison pasty before deciding upon both. Couples entering the supper room stopped to greet the dowager and Dillon, to whom they showed almost equal respect. As if she is handing on the succession to me, Dillon could not help reflecting gloomily.

At the end of the room Caroline sat like a queen amid a circle of young men. Win was at her right, while his two friends, along with the local swains, hurried back and forth offering her choice tidbits or simply sat admiring her beauty like the schoolboys some of them still were.

Across the room in a small alcove, Lord Roxbury was eating supper with a tall, handsome woman who listened to his every word with breathless attention.

"There's Roxbury with his old flirt," the duke pointed out to his mother as he returned to their table followed by two footmen bearing food. "Dashed fine looking woman still, Lady Eleanor, and soon to be a widow judging by the state poor old Bart is in. Roxbury could do worse. She's got two boys. Give that sickly stepson of his a pair of brothers and he might learn to behave like a man."

The dowager nodded thoughtfully. "But Roxbury is not easy to catch. Mrs. Sample, I do hope your pretty Miss Hearn has not conceived a *tendre* for him. No ordinary woman could make a fair marriage with him, though I must admit that he is a charmer. Even at my age, I would find it hard to resist him if he made a set in my direction."

"I have heard that he is something of a rake. His first wife must have given up in despair," Dillon said.

"Oh, not at all! She loved him devotedly, and he behaved with perfect decorum while she lived in spite of her constant ill health. Poor Margarita. She reminded one of a tropical plant too tender to survive in a harsh climate."

"The boy is as bad," the duke agreed. "Never

well. He is certain to have inherited her weakness."

"Perhaps he will outgrow it," Dillon interposed. "How old is he?"

"Near fourteen," the dowager calculated. "As I recall, Roxbury married his Margarita not long after he was wounded at Trafalgar. He had gone back to Jamaica to recover. She was a young widow and Juan was a mere baby. It was some time later, long after their marriage, that he fell heir to the family estates and brought Margarita home to the Abbey to live."

The duke was bored by his mother's reach into ancient history. "Don't dawdle over your plate, Mrs. Sample," he interrupted. "I want to show you the lake by moonlight before the dancing begins again."

"I am far from finished, Your Grace. And I have no intention of deserting your mama while the room is filled with guests. Will you be kind enough to bring me a sorbet? I long for something cool."

"Can't you wait for your sorbet?"

"Randolph, where are your manners!" the dowager said. The duke departed on lagging feet for the tables.

"So!" the dowager said when he was gone. "You're not ready for his offer yet. Or have you made up your mind to refuse him?"

Dillon put aside her hardly touched plate. "I like him very much, but I cannot love him. I am sorry for it. I do not wish to hurt him."

"You have already set your heart elsewhere?"

The dowager was shrewd. Dillon had to fan herself rapidly to hide a rising blush. "I am convinced that I was meant to be a spinster, Duchess. I cannot picture myself in the role of a proper wife."

"No, I can't see you obeying your husband's orders with suitable humility." The dowager's lovely worn face kindled with a smile. "However, I can imagine a husband accepting *your* suggestions, in particular a husband who has already been broken to the leading reins."

"I am not a woman who prefers to dominate."

"Perhaps not." The dowager looked long into Dillon's face and thought her guest touchingly innocent of worldly matters despite her years. "Remember, though, that there is satisfaction to be found in carrying on a tradition and handing it down safely to one's descendants. Love comes and goes erratically, but the land and the family endure."

There was no mistaking the import of the dowager's words. Their eyes met in mutual understanding before Dillon spoke up with her usual frankness. "I am far from ready to make a serious decision. Will you help me postpone it?"

"Of course, if that is what you wish."

The dowager said a few words to a footman who stood close, and in a moment the music began again. Except for the infirm and those guests caught with filled plates, the company hastened back to the ballroom. Even as the duke returned, looking hot and harassed, with Dillon's sorbet, she was already on her way to take her place with Win's young friend Stafford for her partner.

It took some doing, but with the aid of the dowager, Dillon managed to evade a tête-à-tête with the duke throughout the remainder of the evening.

Before the musicians finally put away their instruments, she vanished upstairs with a piteous murmur of an aching head.

"You were shamefully unkind to the poor duke," Caroline reproached her when they breakfasted together in her room next morning.

"No more elusive than you were to Lord Roxbury and poor young Win." Dillon ate a fig with relish. "I have observed your tactics over the years. With the connivance of the dear dowager, I put them to my own use last night."

Caroline stared at her aunt in surprise. "You have changed so greatly since we came abroad that I sometimes wonder if I really know you, Aunt Dill."

"If there is any change, you can attribute it to my having acquired a touch of town polish. Now I am going back to bed. I have sent word downstairs that I still suffer from the headache. Emerald is to bring me a tray of lunch later. When the duke escorts me to the carriage which the dowager has kindly lent us, I plan to look pale and lean upon his arm heavily. He can scarcely read me a sermon when I am ill, can he?"

Caroline stared in fascination as her aunt finished off the last rasher of bacon. "Do you plan to recover when we reach Botham Abbey, Aunt Dill?"

"That will depend."

"If you eat any more, you may not need to dissemble."

Aunt and niece looked at each other and fell into whoops of mirth that left them weak and watery-eyed. When Emerald came in to finish their packing, Caroline dressed for her ride with young Win while Dillon returned to her own room and settled herself comfortably in bed with a volume of poems by the scandalous Lord Byron, reminding Emerald as she did so that she was too ill to speak to anyone.

"Up to something or I miss my guess," the pretty maid mused as she shook out petticoats and folded them neatly into trunks. Miss Dillon would always be wearing that innocent face when she was planning to have her own way in spite of her stern papa or her brother.

If it's that duke she's hiding from, Emerald decided, she can count on me to help! His Grace he might be, but that didn't mean he was good enough for Miss Dillon.

CHAPTER SEVEN

It was a small party that set out at two in the afternoon for Botham Abbey, Lord and Lady Neville having decided that they owed it to Mortimer's betrothed to remain at Benwell with the Daunt family until the following day, when the doctor decreed Henrietta would be able to travel.

Only Arabella Worthing, Caroline, and Dillon, along with Emerald and Betty, Arabella's maid, occupied the dowager's old-fashioned, comfortable barouche as it plodded on its sedate way cross-country to Botham Abbey.

Lord Roxbury had ridden home ahead of them and Sir John Huddleston with him, for they were to discuss the details of the settlement Roxbury meant to make on Arabella which would enable the young couple to marry.

They had been on the road less than half an hour when their coach overtook a runaway cow browsing among the buttercups beside the narrow country lane. It turned a reproachful look back over its shoulder at being interrupted.

"Its eyes are so wistful!" Arabella exclaimed.

She and Caroline immediately fell into a fit of giggles, and nothing would do but that they must stop and weave a wreath of flowers to hang upon poor Bossy's horns. The sky was so perfectly blue and the air so mild and fragrant that Dillon felt no inclination to halt them. After a few minutes she climbed down herself and joined them in picking fat bouquets of the various dainty blossoms that rioted in the ditch along the lane.

They were late in arriving at the Abbey. Lord Roxbury and Sir John were waiting on the steps to greet them. If either gentleman was surprised to see the ladies descend wearing crowns of mayflowers in place of discarded bonnets and exhibiting signs of spring intoxication, they were careful not to show it.

It was another matter, however, when a woman who stood almost as tall as Roxbury emerged from inside and stood surveying the arriving guests.

"What is all this nonsense, Charles?" she demanded. "I must say, Arabella, that I am surprised at you."

"The girls have been a-Maying. They had my permission," Dillon declared, stepping forward. Her own chaplet of flowers sat atop her tumbled brown curls somewhat crookedly. "It was too lovely a day not to be enjoyed."

"May I present my sister, Lady Pomfret?" Roxbury said formally. "You know Miss Caroline Hearn, Aline, and this is her companion, Mrs. Sample."

Lady Pomfret expressed herself as being happy to welcome them, although she looked anything but overjoyed. Dillon, mounting the three wide, shal-

116

low steps into the Abbey hall, reflected that features becoming to a man were not always handsome when bestowed upon a woman.

Lady Pomfret unbent somewhat, however, upon learning of the engagement between Sir John and Arabella. Embracing the girl, she declared that she must immediately arrange a small celebration in honor of the event. Perhaps a Venetian breakfast for a few of Roxbury's neighbors . . . ?

"Please, Lady Pomfret, may we not go on being a small, intimate party of friends just as we are?" Arabella begged. "The announcement will not appear for a week yet, and I want to be at home with Mama at that time."

Roxbury seconded her request. "Give John and Arabella time to make their plans, Aline. Miss Hearn and I will walk with them down to the river while you may want to show Mrs. Sample something of the Abbey. She is interested above all things in matters pertaining to the past," he added sardonically.

Lady Pomfret's strong features showed a hint of pleasure.

"The Abbey has such a long and interesting history that I scarce know where to begin, Mrs. Sample."

She launched at once into the tale of its origins in the tenth century. The two couples drifted off talking among themselves animatedly. As Lady Aline explained that the great hall, which they were about to enter, had once been a chapel where the monks worshiped, Dillon's eyes strayed after the departing ones before she collected her sunstruck wits and concentrated upon the tale her hostess unfolded.

They roamed down narrow stone passages in the Norman part of building, which smelt dank and was not in use, and Dillon peered hopefully into corners in hopes of seeing the ghost of the monk who had broken his vows for love of a lady. According to Lady Pomfret's story, the monk had condemned himself to starve as his punishment, after which his bones had to be buried in unhallowed ground outside the Abbey walls. It was said that he came back often, begging to be shriven of his double sin.

The newer part of the enormous building contained a small family chapel furnished with an early Bible that Dillon examined with awe.

"If it is old books you like, let me show you the library. It is just down this way. Take care! The ceiling is low there. Here we have collected manuscripts over the years which Charles assures me are beyond price . . . Oh, Mr. Forster! I did not expect to find you here at this late hour."

"Lady Aline. Mrs. Sample." The tutor sprang to his feet. "This is a pleasant surprise."

"How is your pupil, Mr. Forster?" Dillon asked after they had exchanged polite greetings. "I hope he is better."

"Oh, very much better. In fact he is here in the library with me somewhere. I have set him to translate ten pages from the *Odyssey* whilst I gloat over our newest purchase . . . Juan, where are you?"

The room was of such a size and dimness except for areas lighted like islands that it was no wonder they had not seen the boy hidden in a corner behind a circle of tall oak chairs. He had been bent over a map which lay on a table under a low lamp when Mr. Forster called to him.

He came forward blushing, a small, slender lad who looked far less than thirteen or fourteen years. His hair was of the shining crows' wing black that told of his Spanish heritage. He bowed with stiff formality to Dillon when his tutor presented him, and her heart went out to him as she noticed how pale he looked despite his dark Mediterranean coloring and how large were his brown spaniel eyes in his thin face.

"You should be out in the sun on such a fair day," she exclaimed after they had exchanged stilted greetings. "Is there not some sheltered terrace where he can sit to finish his translation, Mr. Forster?"

"Señora Mendez would flay me alive if I exposed Juan to the air outdoors. She is the boy's nurse," he explained. "The señora came here from the Caribbean with Juan and his mother many years ago."

"The air is so mild it could not harm an infant. Come, Mr. Forster, and show me a place where Juan and I can sit together in the sun. I promise to help him finish his task while you and Lady Pomfret are occupied with your own affairs. Would you like that, Juan?"

"Very much, Mrs. Sample! It is often damp and stuffy in the Abbey, but I know I must be careful not to catch a chill or I am certain to die of lung fever as my mama did."

"Lung fever is not very common, especially among the young," Dillon said. "I have three nephews near to you in age who are constantly afflicted

119

with sniffles and little fevers, but no one regards them seriously."

"Señora Mendez believes Juan has inherited his mother's weak constitution," Mr. Forster explained.

"Nonsense. He needs more fresh air and exercise, if I am any judge of boys, and I believe I am," Dillon said. "Come along and show us to a place where Juan and I can sit and get acquainted."

"There is the walled garden," Mr. Forster suggested doubtfully, "though if Señora Mendez saw you there she would fly into a frenzy."

"Señora Mendez is rather a Tartar," Lady Pomfret agreed positively, "but it is time she stopped treating Juan like an invalid. I shall go and have a word with her now while you take the boy outside for a breath of air. Really, it is a disgrace how Charles has let that woman coddle the boy. I have told Charles time and again that he should get a wife and give the boy brothers and sisters instead of keeping him in cotton wool as a precious memento of Margarita!"

Lady Aline swept out. Mr. Forster, his arm placed kindly around Juan's shoulders, led the boy and Dillon through the maze of corridors until they came to a heavy oaken door fastened with iron hinges which, opened with some effort, let out into a walled garden planted in herbs and flowers and heavy with the scent of apple blossoms.

"This garden is nearly as old as the oldest part of the Abbey," Mr. Forster told Dillon. "Juan, sit on this bench out of the sun."

"No, Juan and I will sit here with the sun full upon us." Dillon pulled the boy down beside her on a low stone retaining wall. "Juan was born in the tropics. I have an idea that he requires more warmth than English people may."

The tutor looked doubtful. "Go away and study your manuscript for half an hour," Dillon ordered with a smile. Relieved, he hurried off.

Dillon turned around to see Juan staring up at her with frightened eyes.

"Señora Mendez says that unless we can go home to Jamaica, we will both die just as my mama did. She says the air in England is poisoned."

"What nonsense! Air is what we live on. Only smell the apple blossoms! How *can* anyone want to stay inside in a stuffy room when it is like Eden out here?"

Juan's face lightened. "There is a nest in the apple tree. The old tree, there beside the bed of thyme. I look at it from my window. Do you think—dare I go a little closer and peep at it?"

"Of course you may. Climb up and see if there are eggs in it, but take care not to frighten away the parent birds."

Juan stared at her rigidly. "Climb up the tree? I might soil my clothing, madam."

"There are a dozen maids inside to wash it if you do. Hand me your coat and let us see how agile you are. Excellent! You're like a little monkey!"

"Two eggs, speckled blue," Juan slid down and reported. "I have never seen a nest so close before. It is fascinating how they have woven it out of straws and string."

A scream rent the air, so wild and unearthly that Dillon looked behind her for the ghost of the sinning monk. Juan gave a whimper. Following his eyes, Dillon stared up above them at the face of a distraught old woman who leaned from an open window waving her arms and sobbing.

"Señora Mendez is upset again," Juan muttered. "I knew she would be. Now I will have to stay in bed for a week."

"That is ridiculous. She seems to be angry because you have taken off your coat, if I understand her, though I have never studied Spanish."

For the first time the boy showed that he was more than a frightened puppet. With a conspiratorial grin, he said as Dillon helped him into his jacket, "It is well that you do not understand. Señora Mendez is *extremely* angry. She says I might have fallen and broken my neck or have caught a cold in my lungs and it is all your fault."

'What nonsense! *I* might have tripped over that crooked lintel and broken my ankle on the way out to this garden. Or have been stabbed in the back by your Señora Mendez, for that matter. Juan, it is necessary to take some chances if one is to live a normal life."

"I understand." The boy's thin face turned somber. "Sometimes I slip away and play in the stables, but if she finds out, she puts me to bed for days afterward and makes me swallow the vilest medicine imaginable."

"I see. Well, nothing drastic has happened as a result of your little climb today. I am going to insist that you join our small party for dinner tonight. You are old enough to participate in adult society. It is time you came out of the nursery."

The boy's dark eyes, before so apprehensive,

sparkled. He donned his jacket over his thick sweater with a tiny air of bravado.

"If there is dancing, may I watch? Señora Mendez fears I will get overheated if I join in, but I am tired of sitting with the chaperones while Elizabeth dances with Howard. It is time I learned the steps."

"Is Elizabeth very pretty?"

"Like a lily, with golden hair and white skin. Of course she is already seventeen and taller than I, but some day I shall catch up with her."

"Of course you will. Run along now before your nurse falls out of the window. I'll speak to your father about dinner. I am sure he will allow you to join us since we are a small, informal party."

Juan departed on the run after one doubtful glance downward at his sweater, which he had snagged on a small twig. Dillon rose, picked a mint leaf, and crushed it in her fingers thoughtfully as she followed him toward the door. She had seen his kind before, boys who were too sheltered to grow up properly.

The heavy door was still ajar, and she followed several wrong leads before she found her way at last back to the library, where she discovered Mr. Forster, more disheveled than ever, bent in concentration over a scrap of parchment covered with what Dillon imagined was a foreign alphabet until he told her it was mirror writing.

"I am almost certain this was written by Leonardo da Vinci since it is similar to the writing in his notebooks, but I shall have to compare further to be sure." He straightened up and inquired anxiously, "Where is Juan? It won't do to leave him out in the air too long at a time."

"He has gone up to his nurse. She screamed at him from an upstairs window in a frightening fashion. Is she perfectly rational, Mr. Forster?"

"I wish I could be certain. Of course I see little of her. She keeps to the nursery wing as a rule."

"And Juan as well?"

"He is often ailing so it is to be expected that he stays much in his room."

"I think his nurse keeps him a virtual prisoner. Imagine a boy of near fourteen who has never climbed a tree!"

"And never will again, Mrs. Sample!" The library door, which Dillon had not closed, crashed back against the oak paneling. Roxbury entered in a towering rage. "He and his nurse are both prostrated. He has torn his sweater and ruined his boots, and she says he is starting a fever. Kindly leave the management of my stepson to me while you are my guest, if you please, Mrs. Sample!"

"Mrs. Sample was only trying to—"

"You may keep your nose out of this, George Forster. You are as much to blame as she is. Juan was in your charge when it happened."

By this time Dillon had collected her wits.

"I take complete blame for whatever happened. If climbing a low tree to look in a bird's nest is a crime, then it is true that poor Juan committed it and that I aided and abetted him. And yet before you condemn me to your dungeons, let me tell you that I do not believe the boy is naturally unhealthy. He has been so wrapped in sweaters and coddled and taught to fear death that he is on the verge of becoming a hypochondriac."

"He has inherited his mother's frail physique. Dr.

Palliser doses him regularly. I prefer to accept the judgment of a trained physician above yours, Mrs. Sample."

"I simply don't believe that." Dillon's cheeks were rosy with the heat of battle. "All the poor boy inherited was a crazed woman who clings to him because she has nothing else in the world to live for. Juan needs to be out of doors with children his own age. Send the nurse back to her native land and let Juan live a normal life."

"Mrs. Sample may be right."

The tutor would have continued in her defense had not Roxbury rounded on him. "If you spent less time poring over your manuscripts and more with the boy, you might have a right to advise me."

"You need not attack me on that score, Charles. Time and again I've tried to take the boy with me for walks, but Señora Mendez always finds reasons why he may not go. He has a sniffle, or a little rash, or he may be feverish."

"I would be feverish too if I were continually bundled up in several pullovers, woollen undergarments, and knitted scarves!" Dillon declared. "Poor Juan must live in perpetual sweat."

"I see that you two are in a conspiracy," Roxbury said furiously. "You may expose your pupils to the weather twenty-four hours a day when you marry and set up school together, but kindly leave my stepson alone!"

He swung around and departed, not forgetting to slam the heavy door as he went. Mr. Forster looked over at Dillon with an air of pure bewilderment. "I must apologize for my employer, Mrs. Sample. I cannot imagine what has driven him to such an extreme, although Charles has always been known for his tempers."

"It is no wonder, if Señora Mendez screeched at him the way she did at us," Dillon said charitably, "but he does appear to be a man who enjoys ill temper."

"Only occasionally, believe me. I've known Charles Norton since childhood, and the sunny days far outnumbered the stormy ones. It was after Lady Roxbury died that he changed. She was so much an invalid that he felt he should not have—er—caused her to find herself in the family way."

"What an odd marriage it must have been."

"Lady Roxbury was a beautiful woman. He worshipped her."

"I am sure he did. Let us talk no more of this. I need your help, Mr. Forster. I promised Juan that he could dine with us tonight since it is almost a family gathering. Can you manage to win over your angry employer or shall I try myself?"

"Pray let me speak to him! I hope you won't take offense if I say that your presence seems to rouse the devil in Charles."

"I've noticed it myself." Dillon made no effort to conceal a wry grin. "If you need help, perhaps Miss Hearn can persuade the ogre. *Her* presence rouses his angel."

She left the library and found her way more by instinct than memory back to her room, where she shut the door thinking gratefully that there was only this evening and another day to endure before they could escape from the Abbey. Though she had barely begun to explore its treasures, she would be glad to leave the gloomy atmosphere and the tempers of its master.

She wasted no time in going to Caroline's room. The girl sat at her dressing table in a pensive pose while Emerald brushed her magnificent hair with reverent strokes. "What's the matter, Caroline? Are you unwell?" Dillon asked anxiously.

"No, I am fine."

Her smile was dim, as if her mind were far away, and Dillon persisted. "The Abbey is rather gloomy, is it not?"

"Not more so than I imagined."

"Something has thrown you into a mood."

"I believe I am a trifle homesick, Aunt Dill. I miss my own family and my American friends. Arabella is a dear and I'm happy for her and Sir John, yet I feel left out when I am with them."

Dillon caught the wistful note in Caroline's voice. Roxbury, then, had done nothing to forward his suit with her. Either he had changed his mind or Dillon's efforts to thwart him had caused him to hold back.

Returning to her own room, she thought long and seriously while she bathed and donned a severely plain gown which she deemed might serve as protective coloration suitable to the minor role she was to play in the evening's celebration, unaware that the elegantly simple cut of the gown emphasized her erect posture and that its creamy shade of silk trimmed with brown bands complemented her fair complexion and her brown curls.

Caroline appeared withdrawn still when they went down to the great hall together, although she looked lovelier than ever in a gown of buttercup yellow crepe, with her mother's pearls on her throat, the diamonds and sapphires her father had bought her put away to be worn when she was married.

The others were already there. Lady Pomfret wore red satin, which did nothing for her weathered skin; Lord Roxbury, in formal knee breeches and a burgundy satin coat that hugged his muscular shoulders to perfection, nodded coolly to Dillon over the head of Juan, who sat beside his tutor.

"One of the eggs hatched while I was watching from my window," Juan whispered to Dillon after he made his proper bow. "They're already feeding the baby bird *worms*." Catching sight of his stepfather approaching, he added hurriedly under his breath, "You promised that I might watch the dancing later."

"Ssh. I'll try."

Juan straightened up from his bow to give his stepfather a guilty sidelong glance. Roxbury's temper was still brewing within him, Dillon decided, but he made an effort to play the host, sending for champagne to toast the newly engaged couple. After his third glass he offered Arabella and John his own yacht for the crossing to Calais on their honeymoon.

"I am the most fortunate girl in the world," Arabella said, her large, dark eyes wet with happiness. "Dear Uncle Charles, you have been more than a father to me. I dare not say more or I shall burst into tears and disgrace myself entirely."

"Not a great match but satisfactory since Roxbury has made up his mind to give them Morrowfield," Lady Pomfret confided to Dillon. "John's papa is only a baronet. However, his mother, Jean Mackenzie, is a great friend of mine and she will leave him something substantial."

"I hope they will be happy. I met Arabella's mother and found her very pleasant."

"Oh, Amelia Worthing! Pleasant, to be sure, but not at all sensible. She was a beauty once and was still handsome when Henry Worthing left her a widow, but what did she do? Went to settle in her country place to rear all those children on precious little income instead of setting out to find them a new papa." Lady Pomfret downed her champagne and beckoned to Cummins for more. "When *I* was left widowed, even though I was well provided for, I went about finding a new husband at once, and Lord Pomfret has proved entirely adequate. My children are quite fond of him."

"You were very—wise," Dillon responded, with difficulty repressing an unseemly gurgle of laughter.

From across the hearth she suddenly caught Lord Roxbury staring at her with a look she could only call infuriated.

"My dear Aline," he said to his sister scathingly, "when you finish pouring out family secrets to a stranger, will you try to discover why we have been kept waiting so long for our dinner?"

Lady Pomfret bridled and looked ready to snap back at him when they were interrupted by Cummins, who announced that dinner was served.

As several removes followed each other slowly, Dillon thought that this was one of the most uncomfortable meals she had ever endured. A conversational drought fell over the party after the soup.

Mr. Forster offered them a word of his da Vinci remnant, but no one showed any interest. Arabella and Sir John could not take their eyes from each other. Only Caroline and Roxbury kept the dinner from turning into a dismal rout, with some help from Juan, who got up his courage to tell them that there was a secret staircase leading to the cellars, where he had once found a dead bird.

It was a distinct relief when Lady Pomfret rose and led the ladies to the music room. There, over a tray of tea, they discussed Arabella's wedding plans desultorily until the door finally opened to admit Juan.

"My papa says I may dance if I am careful not to get overtired, and if one of the ladies is willing to teach me!" Juan announced breathlessly.

They all rose at once, Dillon to go to the piano, Caroline and Arabella to demonstrate just how a gentleman should address his partner, and Lady Aline to form the fourth in a set. The gentlemen found them busy and full of mirth when they finally abandoned their port and came to join them in the music room. Roxbury's gloom appeared to have dissipated.

"Hold there, Juan. You can't expect a lady to follow such giant steps. Here, let me show you how."

Seizing Caroline's hand from Juan, he led her down an imaginary set as gracefully as Beau Brummell. Sir John hastened to Arabella's side, and Mr. Forster, after a moment of hesitation, was accepted as Lady Aline's partner while Dillon played on.

"What a jolly party after all," Lady Aline panted at the end of a minuet. Approaching the piano, she fanned herself with her handkerchief and said, "Mrs. Sample, it is your turn to dance now. Juan, say good night and run up to your nurse, or she will accuse us of making you ill."

Dillon rose to make room for her at the instrument.

"Change partners, all," Lady Aline ordered. "I am going to play a waltz. Mr. Forster, you take Arabella. Caroline, you dance with John, and Mrs. Sample with Charles."

Roxbury bent in an exaggerated bow before Dillon. She returned an equally elaborate curtsy. As they circled the small room at a decorous distance, with his hand at her waist and hers on his shoulder, she could not help being reminded of the first time they had danced together all those years ago. That was at a party Caroline's father had given at Hearn Hill. Then it was Dillon Hearn who had been sought after. She had only one dance to spare for the young naval officer that the friends of Brendan Hearn had brought with them.

"How very accomplished you have become," Dillon murmured, turning an innocent smile upward toward her partner. "No one would ever guess that you once trod on a young girl's toes so hard as to bring tears to her eyes."

"We all have episodes in our past we wish to forget. The least mention of America makes my hackles rise."

"I am sure it must," Dillon agreed smoothly. "One never likes to contemplate one's wrongdoing if it is possible not to."

"I take it that Mr. Sample never erred. Only a

saint could have survived life with you. No doubt he removed himself at once after his first mistake."

"Since your wife did not survive either, you are hardly in a position to be critical!"

Lady Pomfret wound up the music with a flourish. Dillon and Roxbury glared at each other before they separated to join the group gathering around the refreshment table.

"I have planned an early morning excursion for all except my sister, who does not wish to join us," Roxbury announced as he poured sherry for Lady Aline. "We will leave here at nine, ride cross-country to the bay, and have nuncheon aboard my yacht. There will be conveyances to bring the ladies home afterward, if you are tired."

"What a famous idea, Uncle Charles!" Arabella cried.

Roxbury turned to Caroline, who responded with a smile of agreement. He did not seek Dillon's assent, nor did she offer it, although the prospect of a long ride and a visit to the sea was alluring, or might have been in any company other than her host's.

However, there was only one more day of this painful visit to endure. They were to depart on the following morning. If Roxbury planned the party in order to get Caroline to himself to discover her feelings for him, perhaps Dillon should not stand in the way any longer.

CHAPTER EIGHT

Dillon welcomed Emerald's noisy appearance with bread and chocolate early the next morning. After a sleepless night, she had wakened at six and lain struggling to reconcile her duty with her emotions.

"Everything's in a pelter below stairs, Miss Dillon. There's an old housekeeper has been here since God made the world, but my Lord Roxbury won't turn her off despite she's all about in the head. Poor Mr Cummins, he's the butler, has to oversee the housekeeping and he's almost in his dotage himself, so it's no wonder Lady Pomfret found everything amiss at the Abbey and created something scandalous when she arrived to play hostess for Lord Roxbury."

"Lady Pomfret ought to visit the Abbey more often and help her brother manage his household."

"They don't like it when she does come. She orders things done the way they are in London. They are all hoping Lord Roxbury will marry Miss Caroline."

Suddenly Emerald dropped the fire tongs and sank down on the hearth rug with a sob. Dillon sprang out of bed just in time to rescue the bread she had put to toast.

"Emerald, if they love each other, we shouldn't spoil their happiness," Dillon said through a lump in her throat as she brushed ashes off the half-toasted bread.

But Emerald had no such qualms about showing her feelings. She sobbed wetly on Dillon's shoulder while the chocolate grew cold, swearing she would never leave her darling Miss Caroline even though she knew she would die if she were required to live in a damp, moldy, heathen place known to be haunted by the ghosts of murdered monks.

"Nonsense, Emerald. Ghosts don't really appear to people or we would have some record of the happening. I should love to talk to one, myself. Now sit up straight and use my handkerchief. If it is true that Caroline is in love with Lord Roxbury, and he with her, then we have no right to interfere. You're very young, and I collect that Roxbury has a handsome Irish groom who might help you adjust to life in a new country."

Comforted, her eyes dried, and reminded of her duties, Emerald at last straightened her pretty apron and went off to fetch a tray for Caroline.

Dillon drank a little of her cold chocolate while she donned her riding habit slowly and thoughtfully. She was in no hurry for the confrontation she feared she must face, but it never helped to postpone the inevitable. If one had an appointment with the guillotine, better to meet it straight on than to linger in an agony of waiting.

She set her plumed hat slightly aslant, as Madame Fleur had taught her, and went through to rap on Caroline's door. Her eyebrows flew up in surprise to find the girl still lounging in her dressing gown. She looked tired, as if she had not slept well either.

"It is half past eight already, Caro! I suggest that you hurry unless you want to keep the party waiting."

"Is it so late? I'm sorry. I sent Emerald down to press my skirt again. It was sadly creased from the packing."

Caroline sounded indifferent. She yawned as she rose from her chair and stood staring at the various articles of clothing Emerald had laid out for her as if she had never seen them before. Had Roxbury done something to offend her, or was she unhappy because he had not yet made his intentions known?

"What do you think of the Abbey? It is a handsome property, as they express it here in England, much larger than Hearn Hill and of course more interesting with its long history."

Caroline stepped obediently into the petticoat Dillon held out for her. "It is very impressive, Aunt Dill, but it is not home. I miss Mama and Papa and my brothers more than I dreamed I might."

"Do you like young Juan? Poor boy, he needs affection. I find him a lovable little boy, myself."

"You find almost all boys and some girls lovable, Aunt Dilly."

Pursuing her own thoughts, Dillon continued unheeding. "He will not be a burden, once he regains his health. He'll be off to boarding school within a year or two."

Caroline began to pin up her mass of braided golden hair.

"Poor Mr. Forster. He will be without a calling when Juan goes away."

"You need not worry about him," Dillon urged, exasperated. "He will find another pupil or perhaps remain as curator of Roxbury's collection of books."

At these words Caroline seemed relieved, but Dillon's spirits sank even lower. Caroline and Mr. Forster? Never!

"Has Lord Roxbury made an effort to fix his interest with you yet, Caroline?"

The girl was looking into the mirror, her face half averted.

"Not yet. Not in so many words, Aunt Dilly. We do not know each other well enough to venture beyond what is ordinary."

"I see. Well, there is time yet."

Emerald bustled in with the freshly pressed skirt. Dillon paced back and forth between the windows until Caroline finished dressing. They were the last downstairs, and Roxbury had a frown firmly fastened in place, which vanished at his first sight of Caroline in her blue-frogged habit.

"If you are late, the wait was worthwhile," he responded gallantly to her pretty excuses. "But it is a ride of more than an hour and the grooms are waiting."

Arabella and Sir John rode side by side. Dillon was on Roxbury's left and Caroline on his right as they set off down a long, freshly mowed ride toward the south. Lady Aline had chosen to remain behind at the Abbey to interview the middle-aged maid she had chosen to serve as interim housekeeper, but she had sent a carriage on ahead with a pair of footmen to serve the feast she had ordered prepared.

Juan threw open a window above their heads to wave at the departing company, his face so wistful Dillon was tempted to turn back, although of course that was impossible. Instead she threw him a kiss, causing one of the grooms to snicker and Caroline thereupon to follow Dillon's example in spite of Roxbury's beginning impatience.

The distance proved more than Dillon had anticipated, for which she was grateful. It gave her time to plot her new strategy, for Arabella and Sir John were engrossed in wedding plans and Roxbury addressed all his remarks exclusively to Caroline. They started off at a good pace but several times were forced to control their mounts on passing through small villages, where Roxbury was hailed with a familiarity that surprised her.

"It's our Lord Charlie," Dillon heard a serving woman say, "handsome as ever 'spite o' that scar!"

Involuntarily Dillon glanced toward Roxbury and caught him looking sheepish. Half a dozen men poured out of a small tavern and raised their glasses in a toast. Roxbury threw some coins to them, saying, "I'll join you next time, mates. Drink one for me until then."

A cheer followed them out of that village.

"Your people are exceptionally loyal," Sir John marveled. "I wish you will tell me how you keep them so. Papa is always having trouble with his tenants."

"You forget that I grew up here. As a lad, I sailed with most of the village boys of my age. The men you saw back there followed me to the war. They're old shipmates, and stouter fellows you'll never meet."

"I noticed that one of them had a hand missing and another used a crutch," Sir John said. "Are they able to make themselves useful?"

"In their own ways, yes. If they could not, I hope you would not expect me to turn them off the estate!"

"Of course not, sir. I honor you for your kindness to your tenants."

Roxbury's face turned hard. "Kindness! The man who uses a crutch lost his leg when he dragged me below deck after I was wounded at Trafalgar. The others were hurt or burned when they helped put out a fire on my ship. It is I who owe them more than I can ever repay!"

Arabella, ever swayed by her volatile emotions, spurred her bay to Roxbury's side, her brown eyes bright with tears. "I am proud that you are my godfather, Uncle Charles! There's not a man in England who can hold a candle to you, except, perhaps, my John."

"He may have you back now, Bella. We're already later than I planned. When we reach the top of this hill, let out your horses. Miss Hearn and I will lead the way."

There ensued a short but glorious gallop, which came to an end at their approach to a narrow estuary where they encountered a stony shingle over which they had to walk their mounts to reach a jetty built out into the water. The tide was flowing out toward the Channel, leaving the dock stilts half bare. At the end of the pier, a handsome yacht rode the waters lightly as a tern, its brass gleaming, its decks ashine, its crew standing at attention when the riders dismounted and went aboard.

The ladies were shown below to a salon set apart for their use. It was decked out with rose-colored curtains over the portholes and frilly pillows. Dillon surveyed it sardonically, then was surprised to find herself suffering from a strange pang she could not identify. Surely she was not envious of whatever loose female had made her nest in these rooms?

"Uncle Charles spends more time aboard this yacht than at Botham Abbey or the London house," Arabella informed them as she removed her hat and patted her black ringlets. "My mama says he is a lonely person, but of course he need not be. He is only five and thirty and that is young—for a gentleman." She turned to Caroline, a touch of mischief in her eyes. "Tell me, do you consider that Uncle Charles is old?"

"Of course not." Thoughtfully, Caroline replaced a hairpin in the coronet of braids she wore. "Yet I don't think of him as quite a *young* man. He is strong and assured in a mature way I can only admire."

Arabella giggled. "You sound as solemn as an old woman yourself, Caro. Can we not forget ourselves and just enjoy the day? I am famished, and Uncle Charles promised we would have Jamaican chowder in addition to the nuncheon Lady Aline has sent. His cook makes it better than anyone in the world."

Arabella for once had not exaggerated, Dillon decided after she had partaken of the thick soup. She had a second helping and could eat little of the beef roasted and served cold with mustard sauce or the poached pears and puddings and cakes. The repast was served on the afterdeck under an awning. As soon as it was cleared away, Roxbury rose.

"The wind is perfect for a run down to the Channel. Is anyone subject to queasiness on the water?"

Only Dillon noted the glint in his blue eyes. Surely he was testing Caroline to find out whether she was qualified to become the wife of a seaman, for the wind was steady enough but there was a slight chop on the waters of the estuary.

"I doubt if there is time for a sail," Dillon pointed out. "Lady Aline will be vexed if we arrive at the Abbey too late for dinner."

"My sister knows me well." Roxbury, handsome in his dark riding clothes, lounged against the rail. "If we allow an hour to the Channel and something less on the return when the tide has changed, we shall be home in good time, Mrs. Sample. Miss Hearn, you said you would like to catch a glimpse of France across the water. Shall we?"

Caroline's face lighted with anticipation. Roxbury gave orders. The sails rattled into place, lines were cast off, and the *Margarita* bent under the wind and flew across the water like a bird released.

Three long tacks brought them down the estuary and out upon the restless waters of the Channel. Roxbury handed out telescopes and showed Caroline how to fix hers so that she cried out with excitement upon catching sight of the hazy, distant shore he identified as France.

Sir John told them of his first trip abroad as an aide in Wellington's train before Waterloo. Roxbury capped his tale with a scarifying story of the time his vessel had been trapped in a cove by some ships of Bonaparte's fleet.

"But for a blessed fog that hid us, we had no chance. We put a man ashore with a lantern and a foghorn while we crept out past the headland before midnight."

"What happened to the poor victim you left behind?" Caroline wanted to know.

Roxbury grinned, and for a moment he so closely resembled the youthful Charles Norton that Dillon turned her head away.

"I made shift to cross the headland before dawn to rendezvous with my men."

"Abandoning the lantern and the foghorn?" Dillon wondered.

"The lantern only. The foghorn I used discreetly until I was safe out of reach."

Sir John gave a great guffaw, to which Arabella's light laughter responded in counterpoint. Presently they were all laughing.

The captain approached and asked to speak privately to Lord Roxbury. Only then did they all notice that the wind had dropped. Dillon was not surprised to see Roxbury turn serious.

"We are temporarily becalmed, but you need not worry. If the wind fails to rise, we have plenty of food and water aboard."

"Won't they fall into a panic at the Abbey?" Caroline asked.

"My sister is a hand at sailing. She and I have been becalmed on these same waters a dozen times or more. We used to steal away from the Abbey and sail the dinghy every chance we got."

He has arranged this to get time alone with Caroline, Dillon thought. Excellent! That meant she was relieved of the need to jog him into declaring himself, a duty she had not relished in the prospect.

"I shall go below and rest," she declared. "At my age one grows tired easily."

Caroline managed to suppress a rising gurgle of laughter only with an effort. Dillon had to descend the steep steps in a hurry lest anyone notice her own risibilities.

"There is hartshorn below, my dear Mrs. Sample," Roxbury called after her with false solicitude. "Pray let me know if you require anything else. We do not often have elderly persons aboard, but we will do our possible to make you comfortable."

"Pray do not bother!"

Dillon's foot slipped on the last step. She slammed the door upon entering the ladies' suite and felt somewhat relieved. Of all the odious men she knew, Roxbury was certainly the most obnoxious.

It was not yet two in the afternoon. She wandered around the compact cabin, examined the maid's room next to it, and wondered how to pass the time until the *Margarita* got under way again.

Since it had to be, she found herself wishful that Roxbury and Caroline would expedite their engagement. Now that she was reconciled to it, the sooner they made it irrevocable, the happier she would be, for then she would be free to go back to Philadelphia, where she belonged with Dante and her books—three thousand miles away from the happy couple.

She stretched out on the bunk and tried to sleep, but her eyes remained stubbornly wide open. If only there were a book to read. But when she searched through drawers and cupboards, she found only such comforts as certain ladies might require, such as powder, lacy bedgowns, and even a pot of French rouge at which she raised an eyebrow.

The maid's cabin adjoining was smaller and less cluttered. She lay down on the flat pallet there and closed her eyes. If matters had fallen out differently, if Charles Norton had come back for her as he had promised, he and she would have gone sailing together often, for she loved the water and could have sailed a rowboat to China single-handed with only her petticoat for mainsail, her brother Brendan often said admiringly. They would have shared the tiller when the wind blew hard, even shared the lower bunk in that other cabin, anchored in some quiet cove . . .

She started awake in confusion at the sound of a gentle knock. Arabella peeped around the door.

"Are you perfectly well again, dear Mrs. Sample? My uncle feared that you might be suffering from the motion. He has sent me with a draught to settle your stomach."

"I am not subject to seasickness," Dillon stated, then amended when she saw Caroline peer over Arabella's shoulder, "except on rare occasions. In fact, I am hungry."

"You are always ready for any adventure, Mrs. Sample! Will you come along with us now, please? Caroline and I long to be rowed ashore and walk upon the sand, but we cannot unless you agree to accompany us."

Dillon, sitting up, searched Caroline's face for some sign of heightened sensibility such as a newly betrothed girl might be expected the wear, but saw none. What was taking Roxbury so long! Perhaps, on the beach, she might contrive to separate herself from the young couples and trust the beauty of the blue May skies and the foamy seas piling upon the beach to accomplish what was necessary now.

For it was a golden day. The sun hung suspended above them as the crew rowed them along across a tumbled heap of blue-green water to a narrow strip of land that did not look particularly inviting, although there was indeed sand between the pebbles. The two couples strolled ahead in a leisurely fashion, the girls exclaiming over bits of driftwood or odd seashells they found, which the gentlemen admired politely, while Dillon dawdled along until she extended the distance between them considerably.

"The sun is so hot," she called out, "that I think I will sit in the shade of this rock." When Caroline demurred, she said, "I can keep you in sight at all times so it is perfectly proper. Do go along and enjoy yourselves."

She hoped she had given the impression of being an elderly governess. Arabella seemed to think so, for she coaxed Caroline to come along, and soon their four figures swindled as they walked farther down the beach.

Settling herself against the rock, Dillon waved at her charges when they turned once to assure themselves she was all right. Next time they turned, she pretended to be half asleep. She waited until they were almost out of sight before she stood up and beckoned to the sailors who had rowed them over and who lounged in the shadow of the boat waiting to be called again.

"I am feeling ill," she explained in a tragic whisper to the man who had come at her bidding. "Please take me across to the yacht as quickly as possible . . ."

She let herself go limp. The man sprang to support her. He carried her back to the dinghy at a run, and she was rowed back to the *Margarita* in double time. Unfortunately for her dignity, the giant sailor insisted upon clasping her to his hairy chest like an infant and carrying her up the ladder with encouraging, hoarse grunts lest she grow faint in the process.

"The lady's no weight at all compared to a round o' shot," he confided to the captain, before he was ordered to carry her below. There he placed her upon the bunk tenderly under the eyes of the curious crew. "She's sun-struck, that's wot, bein' a lady and not used to it. Look how red her cheeks are."

And no wonder! But Dillon managed to keep her eyes closed, only allowing her lids to flutter open a little when the captain waved a bottle of pungent salts under her nose. Suddenly she sneezed. Tears ran down her cheeks.

"She's coming 'round," the captain said. "Is there anything I can get for you, ma'am, to make you comfortable?"

"Perhaps a cup of tea . . . ?" she suggested feebly. "I really should return to the beach as soon as possible. It is not at all the thing to leave the young people unchaperoned, as you understand, I am sure."

Captain Keefe, who was not above forty and a handsome man in a rugged fashion, ordered his men topside. When they were alone, the captain studied Dillon with a crooked smile.

"You are not precisely the thing as a duenna, either, ma'am, if you'll forgive me for speaking my thoughts. I'm an old friend of Lord Charlie's so I'll say no more except to add that I've seldom seen a female in more robust health than you are. Did he send you back?"

Dillon flushed a deeper red than the sun had left her.

"It was my own idea." She sat up and pushed back her short curls. "I did it to give Lord Roxbury the opportunity to fix his interest with Miss Hearn."

Captain Keefe's smile warmed his strong features. "You're a duenna after my own heart, Mrs. Sample. Our Charlie has been needing a wife and the young lady is a beauty. Well fixed too, I hear."

"She has the sweetest nature imaginable. If she has a fault, it is in being too kind."

Captain Keefe, leaning against the closed door, appeared to cogitate deeply. " 'Twould suit Charlie better if she happened to be somewhat older, for he's full of tempers and crotchets a girl cannot be expected to understand, but if he's willing to get leg-shackled at last, every man of us will give thanks."

"You don't object to having women aboard?"

Captain Keefe laughed. After a moment Dillon joined in. There was no denying that females had sailed on the yacht before. She was about to ask him about the exotic ports the *Margarita* had visited when they were startled by a shout of warning from the deck overhead.

"Cap'n Keefe, it's Lord Charlie! He's a-swimmin' over all by hisself!"

The captain wrenched open the door, then stood back to allow Dillon to precede him up the ladder until, her pace too slow to suit him, he cupped her elbows in his large hands and lifted her onto the deck in one swoop.

She had barely regained her balance when Lord Roxbury climbed aboard dripping saltwater.

"I believed you were overcome by the heat," he accused Dillon furiously.

"So I was. Now I am a little recovered." She made an effort to appear drooping, which was not satisfactory.

"You should be ashamed of yourself, Mrs. Sample. If you were a member of my crew I would discipline you for dereliction of duty! You are not here to give way to the vapors, but to lend support and companionship to two very young ladies."

He had stripped off coat and shirt on the beach and wore only his wet riding breeches, from which seawater dripped in rivulets and ran across the deck toward Dillon. She stepped aside daintily. Her slight movement infuriated him further.

"When you had to be carried on board, I was sure you had suffered a sunstroke. Instead, madam, it appears that you were simply in a hurry to keep your rendezvous with Captain Keefe!"

Dillon's patience evaporated. "I hardly know Captain Keefe. If anyone is at fault, you are. How *could* you have left the girls alone?"

"They are with Sir John, who is quite capable of taking care of them. Miss Hearn was in such a worry for fear you were ill that she urged me to hasten back."

"You did it for Caroline's sake, then? How kind

of you. She will be grateful, I am sure. Now you had better dry yourself and find fresh clothing before you go back to her."

"I do not intend to go back." Roxbury's scar slanted balefully above his angry blue eyes. "I want to speak to you alone, Mrs. Sample. Keefe, clear the deck! This isn't a raree show. Order the dinghy off, you idiot. Don't stand there with that silly grin on your face."

Magically, in a few minutes they were alone. Dripping but powerful in the dignity lent by his rage, Roxbury forced Dillon to sit in a canvas chair in the shadow of the cabin.

"For you are as sunburnt as a lobster," he advised unkindly. "Now let us have it out. Oh, don't try to deny that you have practiced every scheme in the female books to keep me from Miss Hearn. I have enjoyed scotching your plans until now. I must admit that I'm at a loss. What did you hope to gain by leaving me alone with Miss Hearn, when for weeks you have striven toward exactly the opposite goal?"

"I—I have changed my mind. I cannot bear to see her made unhappy. If you wish to marry her, and she is willing, I will no longer stand in your way."

Roxbury glared at her suspiciously. "Oh no. You can't take me in that easily. You have some devious motive. You want me to offer for her simply for the pleasure of seeing me given a thorough setdown by Miss Hearn. Am I right?"

"How can you be so dense, I wonder? You must have realized that everyone is expecting you to make her an offer. You've paid her marked attentions, and I am afraid that you have won her heart.

Poor girl! Despite your behavior toward me in the past, I yet believed you were gentleman enough not to hurt a creature as sweet and young as Caroline."

"She is certainly beautiful, and kind, and sweet—unlike her aunt! But she is a Hearn. I would as soon marry into your family as to match with the Devil's daughter!"

Dillon's temper caught fire too. "You are so puffed up with your own inherited importance that you are in danger of becoming ridiculous. Do you imagine I want her to marry *you*, of all people? Why, I would as soon she married poor Mortimer as see her tied to a rake who cannot remain faithful for a day! Oh, yes, I was fool enough to wait in the park for you, Charles Norton."

"For an hour, I suppose," he sneered. "When you did not answer my letters, I wrote to your brother. He wrote back saying that you had married and did not wish to hear from me. I can only assume that Mr. Sample came along with his fortune to recommend him above a poor naval officer and swept you into matrimony. How lucky he was not to have run afoul of your brother!"

Salt had dried on Roxbury's muscular bare shoulders and chest, a sight so distracting Dillon turned her eyes away.

"I don't know what you're talking about," she said.

"Your brother might have had *him* kidnapped, as I was. On the way back to my ship I stopped in a tavern for a mug of ale and ran into a pleasant chap who stood me to several rounds of French brandy while he listened to my troubles. I remember nothing more that night. A day later I woke up aboard a reeking slaver bound for Africa by way of the Caribbean. To save my life I jumped ship in Jamaica, where I was lucky to be befriended by an Englishman and his Spanish wife. Margarita was sympathetic. It was she who helped me send off my letters to you."

"I never had a word from you. Never."

"They were the young and foolish love letters of a besotted boy. No doubt you and the wealthy Mr. Sample laughed over them together."

"I tell you truthfully that I never received a letter from you!"

"Then your father and your brother conspired to keep them from you."

"They would never have stooped to such dishonorable actions."

Roxbury smiled unpleasantly. He had the look of a pirate, Dillon thought. "Since they had no qualms over having me kidnapped, I doubt that withholding my letters would have caused them pangs of conscience."

"Please do not speak ill of the dead. My father suffered a fatal heart seizure last year."

"May he rest in peace, though I doubt that he will, considering his sins. He was a dictatorial old bully, too brilliant for his own good, and you grow more like him with every passing year."

Dillon sprang to her feet. "My father was only doing what he believed was best for me when he forbade you the house. How right he was! You would have led me a merry life, with your lightskirts and their pink curtains and pots of rouge!"

He had the gall to laugh. "The rouge was Dora's. She was an actress and as gay a companion as Nell

Gwyn must have been. Unfortunately she had a habit of growing seasick the minute we sailed into the Channel, so we had to part."

"That explains why you took Caroline out today—to test her! Now that she has passed your most stringent tests, I trust you will do what is honorable. Heaven help her if she accepts you, but you have my permission to address her. There. This is what you wanted. Now you have it."

"Possibly you would prefer to do it for me, since you take the girl's business so much to heart. I take it that you have not told her about our former acquaintanceship. You may leave that duty to me."

If he thought to frighten her, he was mistaken. "I shall tell her myself. Pray carry on your own courting. It would sicken me to further this miserable match!"

They glared at each other like battle antagonists, only parting their eyes reluctantly when they heard the sailors in the dinghy hail the *Margarita*. Dillon straightened her small figure and made an effort to smooth her windblown hair. Roxbury lounged back against the rail wearing a smile that infuriated her. Lest she lose her temper beyond reclaim, she turned and hurried back to the safety of the ladies' cabin, where she lay down upon the bunk and assumed an expression of suffering.

"Poor Mrs. Sample," she heard Arabella whisper to Caroline a little later. "Captain Keefe says she is suffering from a mild sunstroke. Her color is certainly very high. Should we bathe her face in camphor water, do you think?"

"Better to let her rest. You go back to Sir John, Bella. I'll sit here and make sure she is cared for."

The cabin door closed. Dillon opened one eyelid fractionally.

"You fraud, Aunt Dilly! You should be ashamed of yourself."

"I was tired. And burned by the sun. You were in no danger so long as you were in company with Arabella and Sir John."

Caroline went across to the mirror and busied herself with smoothing her hair, which she wore today in a high coronet of golden braids.

"I couldn't help seeing that you and Lord Roxbury were in the midst of a quarrel when we approached the yacht. It must have been a serious matter to cause him to swim back and have it out with you. Can you tell me what is amiss?"

Dillon hesitated. "Not quite yet. I took him to task about certain aspects of his behavior. He asked for time to redeem himself and I have granted it." Suddenly she sat up and swung her legs over the side of the bunk with an exclamation of relief. "Ah, we're under way again! Tomorrow you and I must have a long talk, Caroline. Meanwhile, I believe I am hungry. Let us go on deck and find out if there is anything left from our nuncheon."

CHAPTER NINE

The ride back to Botham Abbey was accomplished before the lingering twilight had quite faded into night.

"You are very quiet, Mrs. Sample," said kind Sir John as he reined his horse to her side. "Are you quite sure you would not rather go in the carriage? They are only a little distance behind us, and it would be not matter at all to see you settled comfortably."

"You're kind to think of my small concerns, Sir John, but I am never so happy as when I am in the saddle."

What a delightful husband he would make Arabella, Dillon reflected, holding back her skittish mare so that Roxbury and Caroline, riding side by side, remained a little ahead of her, though for herself, she could not imagine being married to a gentleman who never lost his temper and was considerate of his wife's every mood. How boring never to be able to clear the air with a thundering quarrel!

The evening had turned sweetly cool. She heard

a thrush's housewifely little comments as it settled for the night and was surprised to experience a pang of regret that she had never married. When she had been in charge of her boys at the Latin School she had not noticed the lack of home or husband, for she was never alone. Now everything was changed, the Latin school in other hands, her home henceforward to be in her brother Brendan's house at Hearn Hill.

Until this trip abroad she had been resigned to living as a permanent guest there, for she could look forward to mothering Brendan's three young sons when his wife was brought to bed again. Now she wondered if she could ever trust her brother again. Painful as it was to believe that her father and her brother had arranged to kidnap young Charles Norton and have him shipped to his death on a slaver, there had been so much conviction in Roxbury's voice that the tale must be at least partly true. It could have been done very easily. Brendan knew every ship and every captain, had even hired most of the masters at one time or another, since he was owner of the finest shipyard in the lower states, a man everyone wished to please.

Brendan cherished his hates with the same hearty passion he lavished on those he loved, and he had taken Charles Norton into aversion the first time he set eyes on him.

The fact that Charles was English, was young, handsome, and not particularly impressed by Brendan Hearn had set off his uncertain temper at the start.

"Wretched poor country, Ireland," Charles had

said to Brendan blithely, his eyes fastened on Dillon so that he did not notice that Brendan's smiling face had turned cool. "You were wise to shake off the dust of it, Mr. Hearn."

"Ireland was a lovely country until the English spoilt it, Mr. Norton."

Later, when they were dancing together, Charles had whispered to Dillon ruefully, "I'm ever prone to say the wrong thing. Tell me how to go about winning back his favor, Miss Hearn, for I mean to call on you as often as I am allowed."

He had called the next morning and been received with icy politeness by her father and brother. Thereafter they had managed to meet as if by accident, sometimes in the park, or at a bookstore Dillon frequented, or at parties and balls to which the handsome young Englishman was invited regularly. Their hands had touched and their minds had met, but they had never kissed until that fatal morning when Charles had kissed her to stop her sneezing and her father had found them together.

Dillon's hands loosened on the reins. Her mare stumbled. She gave a sudden exclamation, and Roxbury turned and was at her side almost at once.

"It was my own fault. I was woolgathering," she admitted.

"Your humility surprises me, Mrs. Sample," he said in a voice too low for the others to hear. "You have always been as rigid in your righteousness as your father and brother."

"I intend to seek an accounting from my brother as soon as I reach home."

"When will that be?"

"As soon as Caroline is ready to leave. If I had a choice, I would take passage tomorrow!"

"You dislike what you have seen of England?"

She hesitated, but her penchant for speaking the truth overcame her desire to hurt him.

"No, I find it beautiful in its own way, so neat and orderly in comparison to our wild country. It is only some few of its inhabitants that I have taken an aversion to."

His smile was caustic. "You appear to go on well enough with Burnley. Forster too. Has neither gentleman come up to scratch? I would swear Burnley needs only a nudge to offer for you. If he requires permission from a male relative, I will guarantee to keep poor Neville sober long enough to receive the duke's offer."

"If and when I find that I need help, I will remember to call upon you, Lord Roxbury!"

She goaded her little mare and rode on ahead to Caroline's side. Perhaps she would marry the duke after all. She was smiling at the thought of Roxbury's displeasure when the little party finally reached the Abbey.

An unexpected air of bustle greeted them. Cummins stood in the dim hall wringing his thin old hands painfully.

"Expecting only a family party, my lord, cook made up a simple collation including only three removes."

"More than we need, Cummins," Roxbury assured the trembling butler. "We'll freshen up and you may serve in half an hour."

"No, my lord! Lady Pomfret has already sent

down for the better wines and ordered another course if it can be done. Not enough, my lord, for the duke's consequence, and Lady Pomfret is sadly put about, but we were not warned of the duke's pending arrival."

"The duke? Don't tell me Burnley's here? I am not aware that I invited him."

"I understand that he is on his way to London and finds it convenient to stop here so that he may travel back with your party." Cummins coughed and plunged on. "The duke says that we are to expect Lord and Lady Neville and a Mr. and Mrs. Daunt, with their daughter, and Neville's son for a midday noon meal tomorrow, they being on their way to London also."

Roxbury threw down his gloves furiously. "Botham Abbey is to be turned into a wayside inn for travelers, eh?"

Caroline came to stand beside him, her lovely face warm and conciliating. "Since it is too late to halt this visitation, let us accept it with good grace. I, for one, promise not to take offense when it is discovered that my muslins do not compare with those Miss Daunt had dyed for her particularly in India."

Roxbury laughed reluctantly. "Miss Hearn, if *you* are willing to play second fiddle to Miss Daunt, I can do nothing but receive them with such propriety as I can muster." But it was plain that he was still angry. His eyes coming to rest on Dillon, he turned on her hotly. "Mrs. Sample, it is you we have to thank for this infestation of unwanted guests, I believe. Did you offer the duke a personal invitation, or does he simply follow you as the moth follows the flame?"

Startled by the sudden attack, Dillon managed to collect her wits and reply, "In case you have forgotten, Lord Roxbury, it was *you* who invited all of the Benwell party to visit Botham Abbey when this excursion was first arranged."

"So I may have done, but that was before the Dauntless Bore sprained her ankle and the duke was called on to help out his mama. I had no reason to expect them here!"

"Do not blame me for the strange workings of fate."

"Oh, but I *do* blame you, Mrs. Sample! What is a companion for but to prevent uncomfortable situations? I find you sadly lacking in all the requirements one should be able to count on in a widow of your sort. Of course you are a Colonial and of Irish parentage. I should have been warned."

By this time both Caroline and Arabella had begun to intervene with soothing words. Sir John stood looking on with his mouth open in shock and dismay that a nonpareil of Roxbury's stature should so far lose control of himself.

Roxbury's words quenched any tender pangs Dillon had been willing to admit before. She sprang into battle with vigor.

"What can you expect? You may be surprised, Lord Roxbury. Colonials, you know, are not bound by outmoded customs. Pray excuse me. I must make myself presentable before dinner."

"Burnley is so besotted he wouldn't notice if you wore your shift to dinner," Roxbury sneered, "although why he wants a termagant for a wife is beyond my understanding."

With a cool shrug, Dillon went off toward the stairs. A confused, puzzled Caroline thought she heard her aunt laughing to herself as she followed after her dutifully. Curiosity and concern drew her to visit Dillon's room after she was dressed. There she found the erstwhile widow Sample examining herself doubtfully in her mirror.

"Is that you, Caroline? I've been to see Juan and found him well despite yesterday's revels. Have you any powder, dear child? The sun has burnt me unmercifully, and I have discovered several new freckles."

"You never used to worry about freckles, Aunt Dill. Still I can understand why you want to look your best after the setdown Roxbury handed you! I have come to the conclusion that Roxbury is an arrogant, ill-tempered man in spite of his famous charm. I cannot forgive him for treating you so shabbily!"

"Oh, I made nothing of it. Papa always shouted when he was upset. You will grow used to it."

"Never! I cannot live with temperamental outbursts!"

"Roxbury would never shout at *you*, so you need not fear. Thank you, Emerald. I don't know where you found it, but I am grateful. You had best put it on for me as I have never had anything to do with powder before." When the maid had finished, Dillon stared at herself in the mirror in amazement. "How interesting! It hides all sorts of things. I must

159

try rouge one day when I am not so red from the sun."

Caroline exchanged raised eyebrows with Emerald. Something was afoot when Aunt Dill behaved in that scatty fashion.

The last to descend to the great hall, Caroline and Dillon found the rest of the company standing in a group near the open windows, as far as possible away from a poorly laid fire which emitted gasps of black smoke from time to time like a heaving volcano.

"*Why* they would put green wood to burn I cannot understand!" Lady Pomfret fretted anxiously as she fanned herself and dabbed at her eyes in turn. "Randolph, what you think I shudder to imagine. This household is in need of a woman's hand at the helm."

"Where is Mrs. Wardlow?" Roxbury demanded.

"She packed her things and left while you were gone to the Channel, poor thing. I sent her in the carriage to be sure she reached her daughter's house safely. We are all at sixes and sevens here, Randolph, but as an old acquaintance you are bound to take us as we are."

"Of course, Aline." The duke hovered near Dillon. "I never was a man for ceremony, if you remember. Mrs. Sample, I've never seen you in such a rosy glow of beauty!"

"That's only sunburn, Burnley," Roxbury informed the duke with the jaded air of a man whose hours out of doors only turned him dark as a Hindu. "Aline, if there is a collation to be served this night, may we not repair to the dining room and escape this infernal smoke?"

Lady Pomfret declared to anyone who would listen afterward that she felt as out of countenance among the dinner party of courting couples as a grandmama. Despite her best efforts to maintain some conversation, Sir John and Arabella had ears only for each other. The duke, behaving worse than an infatuated schoolboy over the widow, who was not at all a beauty for she was too slight and had a nose that turned up at the tip, ignored Caroline on his other side.

To make matters worse, her brother Roxbury picked at his food like a spoilt child, complained about the service, and confided his few remarks in an undertone to Miss Hearn, who, though generally considered an incomparable, was not at all the girl she would have chosen for him to marry.

Really, Lady Aline decided, pushing away a bit of jelly that was half-melted, the only sensible person present was the widow Sample. When the ladies retired to the music room, it was Mrs. Sample who complimented her hostess on having pulled the household into some semblance of order and expressed herself as pleased with the dinner. Lady Aline was further gratified to learn that Mrs. Sample had visited Juan before dinner and helped him with his Latin.

Perhaps the duke was not as foolish as she had imagined to set his heart upon the American widow. She wished she could find a similar match for Roxbury. Until she did, she would never be free of overseeing his bachelor establishment, which seemed to be in a constant state of upheaval.

At Mrs. Sample's suggestion, Arabella favored them with some very pretty songs, during which the gentlemen joined them and asked for more. Then it was Miss Hearn's turn at the piano. Her voice was not so fine as Arabella's, thought Lady Aline, but Roxbury encouraged her to entertain them for quite half an hour. When the girl finally rose from the instrument, Roxbury turned upon the widow and said with what his sister thought of as his "impossible look," "Mrs. Sample, it is time for you to favor us. After all, Burnley has not yet had the opportunity to discover how you measure up in the field of music."

"It is kind of you to ask, but I never sing in public. I have no talent for music. Lady Pomfret, I pray you will excuse me. I find that I am very tired after our long day and must retire."

The duke remonstrated. "I wanted to walk on the terrace with you, Mrs. Sample."

"Perhaps tomorrow, Your Grace. I am really exhausted."

Miss Hearn, her young charge, came to Mrs. Sample's rescue, saying that she too was feeling tired. Lady Aline, standing to bid her guests a good night, overheard the duke whisper to Mrs. Sample, "I got old Neville's permission to speak to you, m'dear, and a devilish time I had to catch him sober. I shall expect to see you at breakfast. No excuses accepted this time!"

"None will be offered. I expect to have recovered fully by morning."

Caroline, following at her aunt's side, could not help hearing this exchange, and her sense of foreboding grew. When, at the top of the staircase, Dillon said good night briskly and started toward her own room, Caroline ran after her.

"You can't go off this way and leave me in suspense, Aunt Dill. I know you're spinning some plot. What is it?"

"Why, I simply plan to accept the duke's offer when he makes it. Is that so strange?" Dillon had opened the door and appeared ready to shut it upon Caroline.

"Indeed it is! Aunt Dilly, let me in. I must talk to you."

"Can't it wait until morning? I'm tired and sunstruck and ready for my bed."

"Not yet! Give me just a few minutes, please, Aunt Dill."

With a grudging gesture, Dillon held the door for Caroline to enter, going ahead of the girl to a window embrasure and seating herself there in the shadows so that Caroline had difficulty in seeing her expression. She sank to her knees and took her aunt's hands in her own.

"I cannot believe that you, of all people, would succumb to the lure of a title, not after all the lectures you have given me on the folly of worldly ambition!"

"I'm a bit surprised at myself. It was the dowager who convinced me that there is merit in carrying on a tradition. To keep Benwell Castle as beautiful as it is now will be a task within my scope. I already have ideas to improve it."

"But there is more to marriage than ordering a household, Aunt Dill! I cannot believe you love the duke."

"No, of course I don't. However, I do not dislike him either. He is used to being led, and I am certain that I can persuade him to agree with my ideas."

"You will not always spend your time together discussing your properties. He will expect—I hardly know how to say it—a wife has certain duties which Mama has explained to me. Very *intimate* duties, Aunt Dill, and if you cannot love the man you marry, you might be revolted."

"Oh that?" her aunt asked with a faint smile. "I haven't assisted at the Latin School without learning a great deal about boys and men. I am well acquainted with the means by which all creatures multiply. It's time you went to bed, Caroline."

Caroline stood up, her cheeks pink, and said with dignity, "Very well, I will go, but I warn you that I mean to do everything possible to prevent you from marrying the duke!"

"You may change your mind," her aunt said affably. With a yawn, she slid down from the window seat and rang the bell for Emerald. "Good night, dear child. Sleep well."

"How can I, when you are behaving like a perfect goose?"

"Trust me to manage my own affairs capably. Ah, here is Emerald. Have you been crying?"

The maid tossed her head. "Only a few small tears, Miss Dillon, and those more than the wicked man deserves. Him with the smiles! He's as free with them as his master, they say below stairs, and no more trustworthy. When we go home to Hearn Hill, maybe I'll be nicer to Eric Coachman."

"That pretty apartment in the carriage house

164

would suit you well if you marry him," Dillon said. "Oh, Caroline, are you going at last? Emerald will be in to help you in just a few minutes."

Dismissed, Caroline went to her own room and began to unpin her hair. Bending toward her mirror, she saw that she too had suffered a touch of the sun. And all to no useful purpose, she thought, casting aside a petticoat with unwonted ill temper. Tomorrow she must do better.

CHAPTER TEN

It was a small party that gathered for breakfast the following morning. The wind having risen during the night, a generous fire made the dining room comfortable, and they lingered long over the excellent viands Lady Aline had caused to have prepared.

The duke complimented Lady Aline, but that lady was in a fret over leaving Roxbury's household in the hands of a new and inexperienced housekeeper. "However, I *must* go home to London! Pomfret and I are giving a ball for his daughter by his first wife day after tomorrow. Lydia is a dear girl, though far from a beauty, so that I shall have my work cut out to find her a suitable husband. Do help yourself to more of the game pie, duke. The roast of sirloin is quite nicely done, too, I believe."

Arabella and Sir John were quarreling happily over the number of guests they would invite to their wedding. Caroline, an abstracted smile on her face, ate very little. Roxbury accused her of having slept poorly, and she acknowledged that it was true.

"I had a great deal to think on," she told him, lifting her fine blue eyes to meet his seriously.

"Tell me what I may do to make you happy. I hate to see you in a gloom."

"There is nothing to be done, I fear."

"Don't be a pessimist. I have worked miracles before now."

Dillon was toying with a rasher of bacon and wondering whether the weather was inclement enough to rescue her from the walk in the shrubbery she had promised the duke, when a commotion at the front of the Abbey announced the arrival of a carriage. The duke pushed aside his plate and got to his feet hurriedly.

"Come along, Mrs. Sample. That's sure to be Neville and those confounded friends of his. Girl like a lump of dough and her mama as bad. It's time to see what Roxbury has done with his grounds, eh? We'll leave him to deal with the new arrivals."

"An excellent suggestion," Dillon agreed listlessly.

She had hardly risen before Roxbury got to his feet. "You will be kind enough to stay and greet our new guests, I trust," he said through his teeth to Dillon. "The Nevilles happen to be *your* host and hostess, if you had forgotten!"

Lady Aline struggled to her feet and, with a harried look behind her, went toward the great hall, where the sounds of arrival had risen to a pitch not to be ignored. As if in duty bound, the rest of the Abbey party followed after her, Arabella and Sir John together, Roxbury at Caroline's elbow, and the duke walking closer to Dillon than was either proper or decent, Caroline noticed with disapproval.

I may have to call her "Your Grace" after all.

She is taking to all this pomp like a bird to the air, Caroline reflected crossly.

In the entry hall they came upon a scene of indescribable uproar. Two footmen struggled to hold Miss Daunt upright in a chair while her mama walked beside them admonishing them to take care. Mr. Daunt and Mortimer supported Lord Neville, one on either side. His complexion pea green, Lord Neville, upon being released, sank promptly to the floor and cast up his accounts at the feet of the horrified Cummins.

Lady Neville swooned, though only after she was sure her son was at hand to support her. Lady Pomfret barked out orders to Cummins, to the footmen, and to her brother Roxbury before falling into a mild fit of hysteria, while the Neville footmen plodded back and forth carrying enormous piles of luggage into the hall.

"Roxbury, tell me there is some mistake?" Lady Aline pleaded. "I had not expected—I was led to understand that all of us, including our new guests, were to travel up to London together after nuncheon. You know I must reach home no later than this afternoon!"

Mr. Daunt, his face red, spoke up. "I beg pardon if we discommode you, Lady Pomfret, but there is nothing else to do. One of the horses went lame, almost overturning our carriage. My daughter fainted and is hardly recovered yet."

"You could very well borrow a fresh team from Roxbury," Lady Pomfret urged. "I am persuaded he will not object at all."

"Nor would I," Roxbury drawled, "but Miss Daunt appears to have sickened again. Aline, you may go whenever you choose. Lady Neville is here to lend propriety to our impromptu house party, and we all understand that your duty demands your presence in London."

"As you wish Charles." Lady Aline cast a speaking glance around at the shocking disarray in the hall. "I shall depart as soon as my maid has finished packing."

Except for Mr. Daunt, only Dillon heard the exchange between brother and sister. Caroline and Arabella had hurried to the aid of Lady Neville. Sir John, the duke, and two footmen hauled Lord Neville up into a chair, and several maids scurried around with mops and pails, cleaning up. Mortimer, his own complexion faintly green, took care to ignore his male parent while he devoted himself to soothing the querulous Miss Daunt, who complained that her ankle pained her terribly.

Dillon took in the debacle with a half-suppressed smile before saying aloud, "In Lady Pomfret's absence, Lord Roxbury, someone should make sure the rooms are ready for your guests. Pray excuse me while I go in search of the new housekeeper."

"It is not your affair to oversee the housekeeping here," growled the duke testily.

"Someone must do it," Dillon responded reasonably, "and as I have already talked to Mrs. Brand it had better be me."

The duke caught her by the wrist as she walked away. "You promised to walk in the shrubbery with me, Mrs. Sample!"

"And so I shall, as soon as I have got things sorted out here," Dillon explained patiently. "Now, if you will let me go . . ."

Lady Pomfret had already taken her departure in a mood of high displeasure before a late nuncheon was finally served to the overgrown party. Roxbury surveyed his unwanted guests down the table with a gleam of sardonic humor.

"We are gathered here together at the whim of Fate, it would seem, rather like the shipwrecked folk in Mr. Shakespeare's play. I suggest that we try to make the best of it. Mrs. Daunt, have our servants made your daughter comfortable?"

"I left her resting on her bed. She was still fretful, but that may have been partly due to hunger."

"Her tray will have gone up by now," Dillon assured Mrs. Daunt, earning thereby an unexpectedly black look from her host.

The duke, who had spent the intervening time enjoying Roxbury's finest claret, cried jovially: "Leave it all to Mrs. Sample. Never saw a woman with a better grip on those rum affairs ladies deal with. My mama says the same."

"Mrs. Sample possesses other, more important talents," Caroline said, addressing the duke in a challenging fashion. "In our country she is recognized as a teacher as well as a poet of distinction. She need not waste her time on household problems!"

"Hush, Caroline. Don't reveal my guilty secrets," Dillon chided.

"A poet?" The duke appeared at a loss.

"You must write an ode in honor of our wedding, Mrs. Sample," Arabella said, clapping her small hands together in delight. "You will make us famous for generations to come."

Mr. Daunt stared across the table at Dillon with an air of suspicion.

"I've heard that some few females write romantic novels, but poetry is the occupation of a gentleman. If my wife were to take up writing verses I should quash that activity at once."

"Stamp it out, as you would an insect?" Roxbury inquired suavely.

"Exactly! Don't ever let those things get out of hand or you're overrun, sir. Why, in India, if you let one beetle escape, by morning you will have a thousand of the cursed creatures swallowing down your house."

"Hornby is right," Mrs. Daunt agreed. "Even in the palace at Bharapur, there were bugs everywhere! Although of course the ranee was loaded with jewels that would put those in England to the blush."

Silence ran over the table like an ill wind. The duke, coughing, withdrew a fish bone from his mouth.

"It is not unbecoming in a woman to read, you know," he advised Caroline kindly, "so long as she does not neglect her other duties. My mama has a book in her hand quite often."

Caroline raised an urgent, eloquent eyebrow in Dillon's direction. Dillon, with a slight shrug, launched into a series of polite questions anent the Daunts' proposed purchase of a large estate near Cambridge, and the rest of the meal passed off without further incident. After an exchange of whispers with Cummins, she arose.

"You will want to show the gentlemen over your grounds, Lord Roxbury," she advised, "while we ladies repair to our rooms to rest. I am sorry, Your Grace, but I cannot view the garden with you now as I am promised to visit Juan in his schoolroom. Perhaps after tea? Come along, Arabella. Don't dawdle."

Roxbury, watching them cluster around the door to the hall like a bevy of birds in their pretty muslins, leaned on his elbow and puzzled over what was happening. Matters were not going as he had expected. What was that woman up to? If he hoped to scotch her devious plans, he had first to find out what they were.

None of the ladies came downstairs for tea. In the billiard room, the duke, having missed an easy shot, complained.

"Not the thing at all, Roxbury, putting your guests to work. Mrs. Sample is busy overseeing your household, her maid tells me, and we were to walk in the garden this afternoon."

"Nobody asked her to take command!"

"No, but somebody has to," the duke pointed out. "You ought to marry, Roxbury. I'll coax my mama to look about for the right match, if you don't win Miss Hearn's hand after all."

Mortimer, seeing the expression on Lord Roxbury's face, beckoned to a footman and had his glass refilled. Best go to his room soon, his thoughts ambled inside his head, before that famous Roxbury temper exploded and destroyed him in its aftermath.

Mr. Forster, beaming and rumpled, as usual, joined the ill-assorted dinner party that night. Miss Daunt, recovered from her faint, consented to be

172

conveyed to the dining room by a different pair of footmen, a very large bundle in pink with Mortimer at her side carrying her fan and her India shawl.

The moment he had paid his respects to the other guests, Mr. Forster made straight for Dillon. "It is genuine! I have found a page to compare it with and I was right!"

"Knew what was genuine?" Roxbury inquired, following the tutor with a casual air.

"The da Vinci letter! The one I bought for a pound when I bought the old maps you wanted. It is so rare it is priceless."

"Daventry?" inquired Lord Neville with a stifled yawn. "Can't be from Daventry, that letter. Fellow was killed in a duel five years ago."

"Not Sir Harold Daventry, Lord Neville. I spoke of the famed Italian artist, Leonardo da Vinci," Mr. Forster explained.

"Foreigners! Can't stand the pack of 'em." Cummins seeing Lord Neville's black scowl, hurried a footman across to fill his glass, and the gentleman sank back contentedly.

"We plan to visit Italy on our honeymoon," Arabella bubbled, "do we not, John? Uncle Charles has promised to write letters to his friends in Rome and Florence."

"Rome," Lady Neville complained, wrapping her shawl closer around her scrawny shoulders. "I have never seen a dirtier city."

"Then you missed Naples," Roxbury commented. "Cummins, what is delaying dinner?"

"The duke, my lord. That is to say, he is not down yet, and I thought you would wish to wait for him."

173

"Send Martin up to roust him out. It grows late, and our guests will want to rest as they will be leaving quite early in the morning. I myself have an appointment in town at eleven."

"Yes, my lord," Cummins murmured, and hurried off to dispatch young Martin upstairs. Tossing this clutch of visitors out, or I miss my guess, Cummins ruminated, and to judge by Lord Neville's behavior, they deserved no better. Miss Arabella and Sir John he did not object to, nor even the American ladies, but these new arrivals were not at all the sort the Abbey was used to entertaining in the old days.

Roxbury, having watched Cummins go, sauntered over to Mr. Forster, who was engaged in conversation with Mrs. Sample.

"How does Juan do, Forster? No more fevers, I hope."

"He was about to have his bath when I left him. Mrs. Sample has arranged a place for him at the dinner table tonight. It is time he learns how to go on in company, you know."

"Juan at the dinner table again? It is not at all the thing. Why do you persist in interfering with my household affairs, Mrs. Sample?"

"Lady Pomfret ordered it before she left," Dillon replied quietly. "She fears, as I do, that the boy will be stunted physically and socially if he is kept in too close confinement in the schoolroom."

"Juan is an invalid. Excitement is not good for him. His mother fell into fits of hysteria when she became overexcited."

"Boys are not so susceptible as girls to nervous maladies, Lord Roxbury," Dillon informed her

174

frowning host. "Ah, here is Juan now, looking very handsome."

The boy entered the room, hesitated, then, encouraged by Dillon's welcoming smile, came toward her quickly and bowed over her hand. Lord Roxbury took his stepson around the room and introduced him to the other guests. Arabella made him color up with the kiss she gave him, but he answered the jolly questions put to him by the gentlemen with such eager sincerity that the whole company took him in liking.

Only Dillon, crossing the room to pick up her shawl, which she had left on a table near the door, saw his black-clad nurse standing outside, her face twisted with anguish. The moment Señora Mendez realized that Dillon had seen her, she cast a smouldering glance out of her plum-black eyes at Dillon and vanished silently.

She would love to murder me, Dillon thought, but she can't with all this company present. It's lucky that I'm leaving for London tomorrow.

Dillon had only just moved away from the door, intending to do her duty by Mrs. Daunt, when the duke entered. His weathered countenance was peevish, and he sported a small plaster on his chin where his valet had nicked him with the razor, but his eyes brightened on beholding Dillon in her modest dark brown crepe gown, which nevertheless highlighted her brown curls and gray eyes exactly as Madame Fleur had foreseen.

"Tonight!" he said, holding Dillon's hand too long. "I will not be put off any longer!"

"Very well," Dillon acquiesced, aware that in the

silence which followed the duke's entrance everyone present must have heard their little exchange.

The duke straightened up, releasing her hand, and strode over to Roxbury. "I hope you have some decent wine on hand for the toasts, Norton."

"If I were you, I would not celebrate prematurely, Burnley."

"No need for you to act the high stickler, Roxbury. I haven't asked the lady yet and she hasn't said yes, but you may take it as done."

"It will not do, Burnley."

The duke's countenance turned faintly purple. "Not do? What business is it of yours to say whether or not my wedding this lady will do?"

"There exists an impediment which I prefer not to discuss in the presence of others."

"An impediment . . . ?"

"Mrs. Sample may have made a prior commitment, or so I have been informed."

"A prior . . . ? Why, you are raving, Roxbury. Who gave you the information?"

"I have received a letter from a gentleman who says he will arrive from London this evening to claim the lady."

The Nevilles and the Daunts, intrigued by the drama into unaccustomed silence, sat watching as round-eyed as spectators at a play. Roxbury sipped his wine, looking pleased with himself in a way Caroline thought seemed sinister.

Dillon, now the object of everyone's attention, ignored her flushed face and, turning her tilted nose higher, said to Roxbury, "When you have finished with your tease, I believe dinner is waiting."

As if on cue, a bell pealed. It was not, however,

the gong for dinner. The assembled company waited in eager suspense until Cummins finally appeared at the door to announce in his most doom-ridden voice, "The Count de Courville, and Mr. Gilbert Courville."

How have they found us here? Dillon wondered in a haze of confusion. A moment later, she understood. Gilbert Courville went directly to Caroline, and the girl's face glowed with love when their eyes met.

But there was no time for further speculation. Her old shipboard acquaintance, splendid in dark blue satin and knee breeches and wearing a look of mild reproach, was approaching Dillon.

"So you have regained all that your family lost to Napoleon, Count de Courville?" Dillon asked formally after he had kissed her hand. "I am happy for you and your son, but I must tell you at once that you are mistaken if you believe that I ever agreed to marry you."

"I know you did not, but you gave me leave to press my suit at a later date. When I discovered that you were about to accept an offer from the Duke of Burnley, I had to come and beg you to take your time before making a final decision."

"Who informed you of my intentions, I wonder?" Dillon threw a sharp glance toward Roxbury, who stood by the fire in a negligent posture, a half smile on his face.

"Gilbert and Caroline have been in regular communication since we left the *Artemis*. They plan to wed at Christmas, you know."

"Indeed I did not know! Caroline, how *could* you have formed a secret attachment behind my back?"

"I beg you will forgive me, Aunt Dilly." Her hand in the crook of Gilbert's arm, their young faces shining with the glory of their love, Caroline came across to stand before Dillon penitently. "It is not a formal engagement yet. Gilbert was too honorable to bind me to it before I had my Season, but I knew even then that I could never marry anyone else."

"Aunt?" Lady Neville picked up the word and chewed it over with a frown. "Why do you call Mrs. Sample that, Caroline, when she is no more than a friend of your mama."

"So she is, but she is also Papa's sister." Having gone so far, Caroline did not hesitate to go further. "The real Mrs. Sample fell ill at the last moment and could not come with me. Aunt Dillon Hearn agreed to take her place, but since she is unmarried, Mama said it would not do, despite the fact that Aunt Dill is nearly thirty and quite on the shelf, or so everyone believes in Philadelphia, since she has refused more than one offer of marriage and prefers to live as a spinster."

"Masquerading as a married woman—I have never heard such a shocking tale!" cried Mrs. Daunt. "Hornby, we must leave at once. We cannot allow our innocent daughter to remain among such depraved company."

"But we haven't had dinner yet, m'dear," that gentleman reminded her.

Mortimer surprised everyone with a high-pitched cackle of laughter. "Our little country cousins," he gasped, "have turned the trick on us!"

"I am not amused," his mother said heavily.

"Wasn't that the gong?" Lord Neville wakened

178

with a start and jerked to his feet. "Mus' be time to eat, eh, Roxbury? I'm deuced hollow in the middle, I must say."

"Yes, let us go in to dinner," Lord Roxbury said smoothly. "I have had extra places laid for our two newest guests. The seating has been rearranged. I have placed the erstwhile Mrs. Sample between my son Juan and his tutor in order to forestall any difficulties until we have dined. After dinner there will be time for the lady to decide between her two suitors. Lady Neville, will you give me your arm?"

He swept that drooping woman into the dining room, leaving the remainder of the company to sort themselves out as they chose.

Kind Mr. Forster reached Dillon before the duke or the new Count de Courville and offered his arm. "Do not let yourself be hurried into any arrangement you cannot like," he whispered. "You may count on me to stay by your side as long as you need me."

Juan hurried to Dillon's other side and painfully squeezed the hand she held out to him. "It is an honor to sit near you, Señora," he said in an access of Spanish pride.

" 'Señorita' is the proper form of address," Lord Roxbury corrected his stepson, "now that we are learning more about the older Miss Hearn's past."

Both Dillon and Caroline aimed angry glances toward their host which he appeared not to notice as he devoted himself affably to coaxing Lady Neville out of her sulks.

"Lord save me from ever serving such a dinner party again!" Cummins complained in the kitchen even before the roasts came on. "All of them at sixes

179

and sevens, my lord grinning like a fox, and the duke staring at the American lady like a lad in a sweetshop, and the French count as bad. And the lady chatting away with Master Juan about some Greek called Playto as cool as if she didn't notice anything. Oh, it's a day for disaster! I feel it in my bones, and it's not over yet."

Even as he spoke, a post chaise was pulling up at the front door.

CHAPTER ELEVEN

"I fear you cannot see Lord Roxbury tonight," Cummins told the gentleman who had arrived so unexpectedly. At first tempted to refuse the newcomer admittance to the Abbey, Cummins took note of the man's well-tailored coat and pantaloons and led him to a small reception room off the hall. "Lord Roxbury is entertaining friends at dinner and must not be disturbed. Perhaps if you will return tomorrow . . . ?"

"I will see him now." The gentleman spoke with an air of authority.

"But sir, you cannot . . ."

"I have to get back to London yet tonight and have no time to waste. If you insist on the formalities, you may give him my card."

In the dining room an air of strained civility prevailed. Cummins entered and bent over to show Lord Roxbury the card he held in the palm of his hand with the air of a reluctant conjuror. Roxbury read and his face congealed.

"Send him in, Cummins. One more unexpected guest can hardly discompose us at this juncture."

The man who entered and stood surveying the assembled company had a commanding presence, even though he was short and stockily formed. His thick brown hair, worn in a simple style, was untouched by powder or the curling iron. His handsome face set itself in lines of anger when he saw Lord Roxbury, and he strode across the carpet and addressed his host as if he neither knew nor cared for his host's great consequence.

"Well, Norton, at last! I see you have not learned your lesson even yet. If you have dared to angle for my daughter's affections, I am calling you out, and no rank or title will save you!"

Roxbury rose slowly to his full height, which was half a foot above his adversary.

"Nothing will please me more, Hearn. I have longed to run you through these many years! When may I have the pleasure?"

"Papa!" Caroline cried, overcoming her surprise and running to embrace the newly come gentleman. "Oh, Papa, nothing is as you may imagine! Lord Roxbury has been everything that is kind to me, exactly as if he were my uncle."

Mr. Hearn looked down at his daughter with a bewildered expression. "What's all this? Your mama had word that you have conceived a *tendre* for Charles Norton, who may call himself Lord Roxbury. Knowing the man for a scoundrel, I took my fastest sloop to put a stop to it."

"There is nothing of the sort between us, believe me, dear Papa! I confided in Lord Roxbury soon after I met him that I had fallen in love with Mr. Gilbert Courville during our voyage, and he understood and made certain that my letters reached Mr.

Courville in spite of the difficulties of getting letters to France. It is no use to look at me that way because I am determined not to marry anyone else!"

Young Mr. Courville rose and came to join his promised bride. "Sir, I beg your permission to address your daughter. I can offer her everything to which she has been accustomed and—and more, I hope! I promise to care for her and love her forever!"

The senior Mr. Courville said quietly, "You may know of our firm, Mr. Hearn. Courville and Son, suppliers of chemical products."

Mr. Hearn's blunt features assumed an air of respect.

"Designers of the Courville cannon, as well, I believe? I made good use of your products during the late—er—years. But my quarrel is not with you, sir. It is with this despicable Don Juan who calls himself Lord Roxbury."

"Papa, it is all a mistake!" Caroline tried to explain. "Lord Roxbury is unexceptionable, I assure you. Indeed, if I had not already met Gilbert, or if Lord Roxbury were younger, I might really have wished to marry him."

Lord Roxbury bowed to Caroline gallantly. "If I had been younger, and free, I should have made an effort to win you away from your Mr. Courville."

The Daunts and the Nevilles had been watching the confrontation with avid interest. It was Mrs. Daunt who spoke up now.

"But you *are* quite free to marry, Lord Roxbury, and it is true that you have paid the young lady a deal of attention. The girl's father has every right to call you to account."

"I warned my wife that Roxbury would never come up to scratch, Hearn," Lord Neville broke in, "but I assure you that we did our possible for your daughter. Entertained and all that sort of thing . . . Had no notion she was already bespoke . . . Why, our own Mortimer tried . . ."

Miss Daunt threw an angry look at Mortimer, who pretended not to notice. Roxbury, with a contemptuous glance at those seated around his table, called for silence.

"It appears that there are certain questions to be sorted out, preferably without an audience. Miss Hearn, will you and your father join me in the music room?"

Gilbert Courville, who stood at Caroline's side, protested.

"You cannot exclude me, sir. I won't leave Miss Hearn to face her father's wrath alone."

The duke and the new Count de Courville crowded around Roxbury, each demanding a word with Mrs. Sample's brother. Mr. Brendan Hearn, his feet planted apart as if he stood on deck in a stormy sea, appeared at a loss.

"Bless my soul, what has happened here? Is everyone May-mad to be wishing to marry? I cannot distinguish which one wants to wed which lady. Caroline, are all these gentlemen dangling after you?"

"No, Papa." Caroline cast a speaking glance at Dillon, who remained seated in her chair between Juan and Mr. Forster in an unwontedly mouselike fashion. "The Duke of Burnley and Count de Courville wish to offer for Aunt Dilly."

Brendan Hearn brushed at his thick brown hair,

which was so like his younger sister's, staring at her in bewilderment.

"But Dillon don't want to marry. When that Norton fellow jilted her she made up her mind she'd have naught to do with men again." He turned accusingly toward Roxbury. "It's your fault, you faithless rogue. You ruined my sister."

"I did nothing of the sort. I loved her. It was you who tried to ruin *me*. I might have died aboard that filthy slaver you had me shipped on had I not swum ashore at Kingston. There I was befriended by an Englishman and his wife who nursed me through a near fatal fever. Thanks to them I was able to gain back my commission and join the battle against Napoleon. I never had an answer to the many letters I addressed to your sister. Come, Hearn—let us have the truth after all these years. What did you do with my letters?"

Brendan Hearn had the grace to look ashamed. "My father intercepted them. He didn't want Dillon to marry, especially not an Englishman. If we did wrong, then I owe you an apology, no matter that it comes hard to me to offer it."

"No apology can make up for the years lost out of my life, Hearn. You must have wished me dead when you had me put aboard that slaver."

"I had nothing to do with a slaver! I told Boone to get you a bit befuddled in that tavern, hoping your commanding officer would keep you safe in the brig until your ship left our harbor. If you wound up on a slaver, I can only believe that you were kidnapped by some unscrupulous fellows as you made your way back to your ship."

Cummins, who had ordered the plates removed,

stood listening transfixed. So did the newest footman, who, upon hearing that Lord Roxbury had been pressed aboard a slaver, dropped the tray he carried and stood with his mouth open expecting to see his master and the American gentleman engage in a duel.

Roxbury waved at Cummins. "Enough! Clear away, Cummins, and see that the next course is served. Hearn, will you and your sister kindly join me in the music room, where we may discuss this matter in decent privacy?"

"Not without me, Papa," Caroline declared.

"Nor without us," both Courvilles said simultaneously.

"You're not leaving me out!" the duke said angrily. "You may not know, Mr. Hearn, that your sister has agreed to hear my suit."

"I asked her first," Count de Courville said hotly, "and she agreed to think on the matter."

Lord Roxbury folded his arms across his waistcoat and glared down the table at Dillon.

"It would appear that our chief problem is the lady. Mrs. Matilda Sample, or Miss Dillon Hearn, whichever you choose to call yourself, you are caught in a bind of your own making. Be so kind as to choose between these two gentlemen and let the rest of us get on with our dinner. Which will it be? Don't sit there with that stubborn look on your face. Speak up, Miss Hearn, and put an end to our suspense."

"I—I do not wish to marry anyone at all! I am grateful for your regard, gentlemen, but it is as my brother told you—I will never wed."

"You might have informed me sooner," the duke

cried, incensed, "and saved me the trouble of dangling after you all this time! Are you quite sure you won't change your mind?" he added on a wistful note.

"Quite sure. I love Benwell and admire your mama enormously, but it will not do, Your Grace. And Mr. Courville, I wish you every happiness in your newly won estates in France."

"I have no intention of settling there," that gentleman hastened to assure her. He had gained a bit of weight since she had seen him aboard the *Artemis*, which the French cut of his coat emphasized, but Dillon saw that he had not lost his kindly expression nor his ready smile. "Our home will always be in America. We have put such property as was not devastated in the war into the care of a cousin. I shall drop the title if it does not please you."

How, Dillon wondered frantically, does a lady go about fainting? She could not think of how else to escape from the predicament she found herself in. And all of it taking place under Roxbury's amused eyes! Nothing could be more painful.

To her vast relief, a commotion in the hall announced new arrivals.

"If another suitor has come, Cummins, tell him he will have to wait," Roxbury ordered. "I intend to finish my dinner. Martin, have places set for these new guests. Juan, your eyes are as big as an owl's, and you have eaten very little. Señora Mendez will be angry."

"She is always angry, sir, and I am too old to have a nurse. Can we not send her back to Jamaica, where she will be happy?"

Loud voices resounded outside in the hall. "Is this Bedlam or Botham Abbey?" Roxbury complained. "*Now* what is it, Cummins?"

"The Duke of Burnley's son is calling, my lord, with two friends. They have brought a gift for Miss Arabella."

"What kind of gift, Cummins? Why do you pull that long face?"

"An engagement gift, my lord, or so they informed me. In a large bag."

"Oh, what can it possibly be!" Arabella rose from her place at the table and ran past Cummins into the hall. A moment later they heard her give a little scream. With this, the entire party rose, except for Miss Daunt, who shrugged and returned to her jellied capon.

The scene Dillon came on was beyond belief. The three young men, all thoroughly foxed, had let loose a number of small animals that scampered frantically over the feet and through the legs of the bewildered company. The hubbub had reached such a peak that Dillon did not hear one of the little creatures squeal until it was caught in the folds of her skirt. Across the hall Mrs. Daunt screamed uninhibitedly.

"An animal has attacked me. Oh, Hornby, save me!"

"It is only a piglet, Mrs. Daunt," the Duke of Burnley shouted in exasperation before turning upon his son with such a fierce look that Win and his friends stopped laughing and gathered in a defensive knot near the door. "You've been into my claret, you young scoundrels! I'll make you suffer for this!"

"It was only a joke, Papa. You know how Arabella and I have teased each other since our school days. When she told us she and John were to live at Morrowfield and become farmers, we decided to help them make a start."

"Where did these piglets come from? If you have robbed one of my tenants . . . !"

"We bought them, sir, and they cost a pretty penny. We could have given Arabella a silver candlestick at half the price, eh, Stafford?"

Juan gave a triumphant shout. He had been running around the hall on the trail of a plump piglet which he had finally got into a corner and made captive, to the detriment of his fine satin breeches. A stream of advice came from Arabella, Lord and Lady Neville, and the Daunts, who had by now retreated ignominiously behind the dining room doors whence they took turns peering out.

Dillon found herself aided by both the Courvilles. She managed with their help to coax a second frightened porker inside a hastily erected cage of cushions and chairs. Brendan Hearn made no bones about his delight in the scene taking place in the famed hall of Botham Abbey, laughing with such uninhibited pleasure that he had to pull out his linen kerchief and wipe his eyes before declaring to his host that he had never seen anything funnier on the stage.

"Indeed?" Lord Roxbury replied frostily, his eyes upon a small creature just emerging from its hiding place beneath a table. With a smothered exclamation of satisfaction he threw himself to his knees across the path of the third piglet. The little animal cried so heartrendingly upon finding itself a prisoner that the ladies begged Roxbury to release it, whereupon he wrapped it in his kerchief and handed it to a footman, whose face turned scarlet with dismay.

"Thank you, my lord," he gulped. "What shall I do with him, my lord?"

"See if we have an apple. If so, carry him to the cook and have him roasted."

A storm of feminine protests erupted. Lord Roxbury rose and, having accepted Cummins's aid to dust himself off, said to his butler, "Call in a pair of boys from the stables and have them bring enough sacks to hold Arabella's wedding gift. How many . . . ?"

"A round half dozen, sir," Win confessed.

"So few? Your pockets must be to let, Winfield. Ah well, Arabella, they are bound to grow and multiply as no silver candlestick would have done. Cummins, do we have room at the table for three more? No? In that case you may serve some sort of collation to the young people in the music room, but no wine."

Dillon rose up clutching the piglet which she had managed to coax into snuffling acquiescence. "I shall chaperone them."

"Nonsense." Lord Roxbury removed the piglet from her hands and gave it to Stafford, who stood near. "I fear for the direction of your mind, Mrs. Sample-Hearn, if you cannot trust six young men and women to be in company together for a short time."

The young people trailed off together, laughing. Among those left in the hall was the new Count de Courville. Having bade his son a private good-bye, he addressed Lord Roxbury with a certain formality, saying that he was returning at once to the Monkshead Inn, where he and his son had taken rooms for the night. Next he went to Dillon. With a deep bow, he told her that he was her servant, and should she have a change of heart, she need only send word by Gilbert.

Mr. Forster went off to the library to attend to his precious da Vinci relic. Mortimer and Sir John hesitated until Lord Roxbury offered his arm to Dillon before they trooped back into the dining room.

"It has all gone cold," Miss Daunt informed them sadly.

"I have lost my little appetite entirely," Mrs. Daunt declared, although the plate in front of her was empty. "Pigs at Botham Abbey! No one will believe it. I shall never be able to forget this night."

The duke, who had followed his son and friends into the music room, now stood in the doorway, his bony face grim and his color high.

"Nor will I," he said coldly. "Roxbury, I'm off for Benwell as soon as my man can pack up. I bid you all farewell. You too, Mrs. Sample."

Cummins rushed the service of sweets and fruit. Juan gobbled up his own share happily and had started on Dillon's before Lord Roxbury noticed and ordered the boy off to bed.

"Leave us at once, John."

The boy's face radiated joy. "You called me John, as if I am an English boy!"

"So you are. Now go along."

Juan made his bows politely. Brendan Hearn, who had gone with his daughter Caroline to the music room to talk with young Gilbert Courville at her request, now entered and, without waiting to be invited, took the chair at Dillon's side which Juan had vacated.

"I must say I never saw you looking better, Dillon. You've got rid of that bird's nest of hair—that's it! Papa would have fallen into a temper if he had seen you without your braids, but for myself—well, I approve."

"How kind of you, Brendan." Dillon was not so easily appeased. "I trust you can explain to me why you and Papa behaved in such a piratical fashion toward Lord Roxbury."

Brendan Hearn's color heightened. "Papa didn't want you to marry. After Mama died he came to depend upon you. He could not bear the idea that you might remove to England, of all places hateful to him."

"That is a feeble excuse for what you have done."

"I can only promise you that I have regretted it bitterly and beg you to forgive me. I hope it is not too late to mend matters."

Dillon sat up straight. "Far too late. I have learned to enjoy my single life and mean to continue it."

"A more unlikely spinster, after tonight's events, is beyond my imaginings, sister. But you were always stubborn. You never would take my advice, but I hope that if you change your mind, you will admit it. Now I must get back to London, for I have business to attend to there first thing tomorrow morning. After it is finished I will call upon you at Neville House and arrange for our voyage home."

He did all that was proper toward the Nevilles and the Daunts and even made a stiff expression of thanks to Lord Roxbury before he strode out of the room with his rapid walk.

Silence descended upon the table. Lord Roxbury tapped with his fingers, watching the Daunts munch through an assortment of tarts and puddings the cook had sent in as a last desperate sop.

"I feel certain you ladies will wish to retire early," he said, "after this unhappy evening. Neville, if you and your son and Mr. Daunt want to linger here, Cummins will bring in brandy and tobacco. I, however, have certain affairs to set in order before I leave for London in the morning. I beg you to excuse me." He came to a full pause. "Mrs. Sample-Hearn, I require your help, since you have already had dealings with my new housekeeper."

"I have a duty to my niece in the music room."

"In this emergency, duty must wait."

Mortimer watched the erstwhile widow leave the room with a speculative look. Both her suitors were men of wealth and title, and now it appeared that Roxbury might enter the field. Odd to see them dangle after a female who had been on the shelf for years. Of course she was lively and accomplished and very interesting to converse with, but to think of Lord Roxbury wed to a woman who wrote verses boggled the mind.

Dillon and Roxbury had not yet reached the door when a loud altercation from the hall informed them that the Duke of Burnley was taking his departure, though not before he showered a storm of acrimonious words upon his son's head.

Roxbury waited until the commotion subsided. At his side, Dillon thanked the gods that Burnley had not taken time to upbraid her as well as his son.

She was conscious of feeling peculiar: she was hot and cold by turns, and her stomach fluttered as if she were at sea again. It was with relief that she saw Cummins approaching. She entered into a low-voiced colloquy with the butler, after which she said, "A tea tray will be sent to your rooms, Lady Isabel and Mrs. Daunt. Cummins has two footmen ready to carry Miss Daunt up whenever she is ready. Lord Roxbury, I will meet you in the office after I have been up to the nursery. Juan's Señora Mendez sends word that she must speak to me at once about the boy."

Lady Isabel gave an audible click of the tongue. "It is hardly suitable for an unmarried woman to give orders in a bachelor establishment!"

"Very odd indeed," Mrs. Daunt agreed emphatically. "It would never be tolerated in India, I assure you."

"Then it is fortunate we are living in a more civilized country," Roxbury said coolly, before turning to Dillon. "Ten minutes, no more."

Dillon escaped with a nod of assent and a prayer of thanks. If Roxbury meant to castigate her family, at least it would be one in the privacy of the office. She supposed she owed him the opportunity, after what the Hearns had done to him.

She darted lightly up the steps. It was to be hoped that Juan had taken no ill from the excitements of the past days. His cheeks had glowed with color, and he had eaten with some gusto at the end of the dinner, which was unusual for him. Perhaps he was experiencing a stomach upset. If so, she had certain powders along which she could give him.

She scratched twice on the door of the schoolroom

before it opened a crack to show the dark-ringed eyes of Señora Mendez peering out at her.

"I came in answer to your message, señora. I hope Juan is all right?"

"He is not bad tonight. It is you I wish to speak to. Come inside."

Dillon edged uneasily through the slight opening the nurse made for her. "Juan ate a good many cakes at dinner. If he has had a little upset, it is no wonder. Boys are apt to overeat, you know."

The woman made no answer, only motioning to Dillon to go ahead of her toward the hearth, where a robust fire glowed. The room was in almost total darkness, its windows shut against the mild May evening and heavy curtains drawn. With a gesture at once humble and imperious, the old nurse pointed Dillon to a seat upon a bench beside the fire.

"That is where my mistress always sat. Juan's mother was a beautiful woman. It was a great sorrow to her family when she, a widow, married milord Roxbury and took their grandson away from them. Juan has never been strong since he came to this terrible land. He will die unless he goes home to the country of his birth!" The woman's black eyes had fastened on Dillon like a pair of leeches.

"He appears to be as strong as the average lad of his age, señora. Growing boys have a way of turning lanky and suffering from colds and bad throats, but you'll see him outgrow it in a year or two."

"How can you know? You are not his mother. You have no child of your own. You say the easy, happy words Lord Roxbury used to coax our little Margarita from her home, where she was well and happy.

195

Here she died from the cold before two years were out."

"I thought she died in childbed, Señora Mendez."

"Margarita could not stop coughing, and the little one came too soon."

"I am truly sorry, señora—sorry for your lovely mistress and the baby as well. And for Lord Roxbury, because he must miss Lady Margarita."

The woman, who had been kneeling before the fire, picked up an iron poker and pushed back a glowing log that threatened to fall onto the hearth.

"Milord shows his grief in a strange way. Oh, do not believe you are the first woman he has brought here, madam—or the last! The light women were not of any matter, but I know my mistress can never sleep in peace if milord marries a new wife." The woman stood up suddenly, the hot poker grasped in both her hands. "I have made a vow to prevent it."

Dillon half rose, the blood singing in her ears. The old nurse was mad, and she stood between Dillon and the door. Señora Mendez must weigh half again as much as she, Dillon thought hastily, which ruled out any chance of besting her in hand-to-hand combat. She would have to try to talk her into rationality.

"I have no intention of marrying Lord Roxbury, nor does he wish to marry me, if that is what you believe, Señora Mendez. You are alarming yourself needlessly over a situation that will never occur."

"Milord will win you around. He is clever and he can be charming when he wishes, that devil milord! But I will make sure that he does not try. It will hurt only a little. Only a little!"

The point of the hot poker swung toward her face

so suddenly that Dillon was able only to turn to one side. Even while she screamed for help, she felt the heat of the iron sear her shoulder through the thin stuff of her gown.

"Mrs. Sample!" It was Juan's high, anguished voice. He came running from the adjoining room and began to grapple with Señora Mendez. "If she has hurt you . . . ! Stay back—I can handle her. Señora, listen. It is only your Juan. You cannot want to hurt your Juan. Put down the poker and I will send for wine and we will talk together all about Mama."

The old woman began to wail in eerie tones that sent chills along Dillon's spine. Juan took the poker from her and began to lead her away when the door from the hall burst open to admit Lord Roxbury, followed by Cummins and Gilbert Courville.

Dillon sank down upon the settee, but before she could lean back, Roxbury scooped her up into his arms. "Is the pain bad?"

"I can bear it. I'll go to my room."

"Lie still and be quiet." Over her cradled body she heard Roxbury issue a series of terse commands, to Juan to lead the nurse to her room and ring for a maid to attend her, to Cummins to summon the physician at once, to Gilbert Courville to fetch Caroline to help with her aunt.

Despite the increasing pain in her burnt shoulder, Dillon felt a sensation of lightness, a mad sort of euphoria. It's due to shock, she warned herself. Nevertheless she was aware of every quick beat of Charles Norton's heart, of the scent of his linen, and of the warmth of his body as he set off down the hall in the direction of her room.

She could not help wincing when her back touched the coverlet of her bed.

"Turn onto your left side," he ordered. When Emerald hurried in uttering loud lamentations, he bade her to be quiet. "Go and bring me clean cloths and a basin of cool water. First, scissors. We'll have to cut away the fabric around the burned area." The cloth parted from Dillon's blistered flesh reluctantly. She could not repress a small moan. "Will you hurry with those cold cloths!" Lord Roxbury roared at the maid, whose hot tears were dripping freely upon Dillon's scalded skin.

Caroline came running in as Emerald departed. Sensible, good girl, Dillon reflected as she heard her niece set about finding soft linen for a bandage.

"Will it leave a scar?" Caroline inquired of Roxbury.

"I'm afraid it will, but that is our least concern. We must take care not to let the raw flesh become infected. Where is that doctor?" he fumed.

A bandage in place, Dillon surprised them both by sitting up abruptly. "I am not subject to infections. I've always been revoltingly healthy," she informed them. Before either one could speak, she rolled across to the far side of the bed and slid down to the floor. "You see? I am quite able to take care of myself."

Awakening the next morning, Dillon blushed for her own brash foolhardiness. How humiliating to swoon in front of Caroline after all her caustic remarks about fainting females! Even worse it was to show any sign of weakness before Roxbury, her bitter enemy!

She had a vague memory of being given a dose of laudanum by the doctor. Feeling under the covers, she was reassured to learn that she was decently attired in her nightdress. Emerald must have put it on her. Afterward—surely it was a nightmare—she thought she had been kissed and tucked under her linen sheet by Lord Roxbury.

She ought to get up at once and prepare for the journey back to London, she told herself, but it was too much of an effort to summon Emerald. Instead she drifted off into a dreamy langour, waking only when a rustle of skirts and a cool hand on her forehead let her know that Caroline was there.

"What time is it, Caro? We had best hurry if we are to reach London by noon."

Looking even more golden and beautiful than usual, if such could be, Caroline leaned down to kiss Dillon softly. "It is past eleven, Aunt Dilly." She was smiling. "The Nevilles and the Daunts have long since gone. Dr. Parsons has decreed that you are to remain quiet for a day, although you may get up and dress later if you feel well enough."

"I suppose Roxbury has gone, too? I recall that he spoke of an appointment in the city this morning."

"Of course he has not left. He is waiting outside the door to learn how you are this morning."

"Tell him I'm perfectly well." Dillon made a move to sit up and sank back again. "Except for a slight discomfort in my shoulder. He need not delay his return to the city because of me. I can be ready to leave within the hour."

Caroline was amused about something and did

not trouble to hide her smiles. "I think you had better tell him yourself."

The door flung open, and Roxbury marched across the Persian carpet to stand by her bedside with a fierce scowl.

"Of all the stubborn, birdbrained females I have known, you win the laurels! First you offer yourself to Señora Mendez like a lamb to the sacrifice. Then, after you have endured shock and a serious burn, you are idiotic enough to jump out of bed and fall senseless before I can save you! Am I so terrifying that you are afraid to stay in my house?"

"Yes," Dillon replied, not looking at him. "If I am so feeble, you should not be shouting at me this way."

"This is too much!"

Roxbury suddenly tossed away the comforter under which Dillon nestled and snatched her out of her bed in one eaglelike swoop.

"You have taunted me one too many times, Miss Dillon Hearn! With your beloved niece as witness, I intend to kiss you. If you truly despise me, you need not respond, in which case I promise to return you to your bed and call for the coach to take you back to Neville House. My intentions, God help me, are honest, I should state before we begin."

"I do hope so, Lord Roxbury," Caroline remarked with her famous smile, "for I am exhausted with the effort of chaperoning my beloved, but difficult aunt. I will be only too happy to turn over my duty into your hands."

"Caroline!" cried Dillon in the tone of one betrayed.

She had the words ready to accuse her niece of

200

desertion before she found her lips stopped with the kiss Roxbury had threatened, and she foundered in bliss. When she turned her face from his at last to draw a breath, she discovered Caroline was gone.

Primly, she said, "We are alone and I am wearing only a bedgown. Caroline should not have left."

"Shall I ring for your maid?"

She sneezed twice. "No, though you may put me back into bed when you have finished kissing me."

"You do grow exceedingly heavy. I see no reason why we can't go on kissing while I am seated in the chair by the fire, not that you have finally put aside your maidenly scruples. By the way, I have applied already for a special marriage license. I have no intention of letting you escape again."

She looked up into his face, so changed and yet so familiar despite the cruel scar, and said, marveling, "Why would you marry an aging school teacher who never had any pretentions to beauty, I wonder?"

His eyes lighted with the devilish glint of humor she never could resist. "Because you know all about drains, and I can count upon you to manage my estates and cosset me in my old age." He caressed her cheek gently. "Though not until we arrange for an heir or two, I think." He gave a shout of laughter. "I was sure that would bring up a blush!"

"I am not accustomed to sit upon a gentleman's lap in my bedgown, please remember! If you wish me to learn new arts, you will have to introduce me to those acquaintances of yours who leave their rouge pots aboard the *Margarita*."

"Whatever you need to learn I intend to teach you myself." Roxbury held her a little away from his chest and looked down into her face for a long moment. "It would not surprise me to discover that I have more to learn than you do about the secrets of love."

"You may count upon me to tutor you," she agreed gravely.

Suddenly they were laughing together, like a pair of children, thought Caroline as she peered through the door at them, and her lips curved into a tender smile. She tiptoed away.

Gilbert and I will visit them every other year, she decided, between their visits to us. Meanwhile she had best start looking around for a suitable wife for Gilbert's papa, since he could not have Aunt Dilly. Matchmaking was wonderful fun.